WORSHIP ME
IMMORTAL VICES AND VIRTUES

AURELIA JANE

KEL CARPENTER

Worship Me

Kel Carpenter and Aurelia Jane

Published by Raging Hippo LLC

Copyright © 2022, Raging Hippo LLC

Cover Art by Yocla Designs

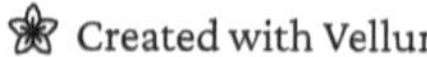 Created with Vellum

ABOUT THE AUTHORS

Kel Carpenter and Aurelia Jane are the hilarious team behind the international bestselling series, A Demon's Guide to the Afterlife.

They pride themselves in being absolute weirdos, spending hours on the phone coming up with detailed worlds, and laughing about crazy ideas for torturing characters. While they believe they each have the personality of a rabid badger, people still seem to like them okay.

They share a love of coffee, travel, and tacos, and they've made some adorable tiny people with their equally weird husbands. Best friends and work wives, Kel has the audacity to live in Maryland while Aurelia lives in Texas, but they try to see each other as much as possible.

Join Kel and Aurelia's Readers Group!

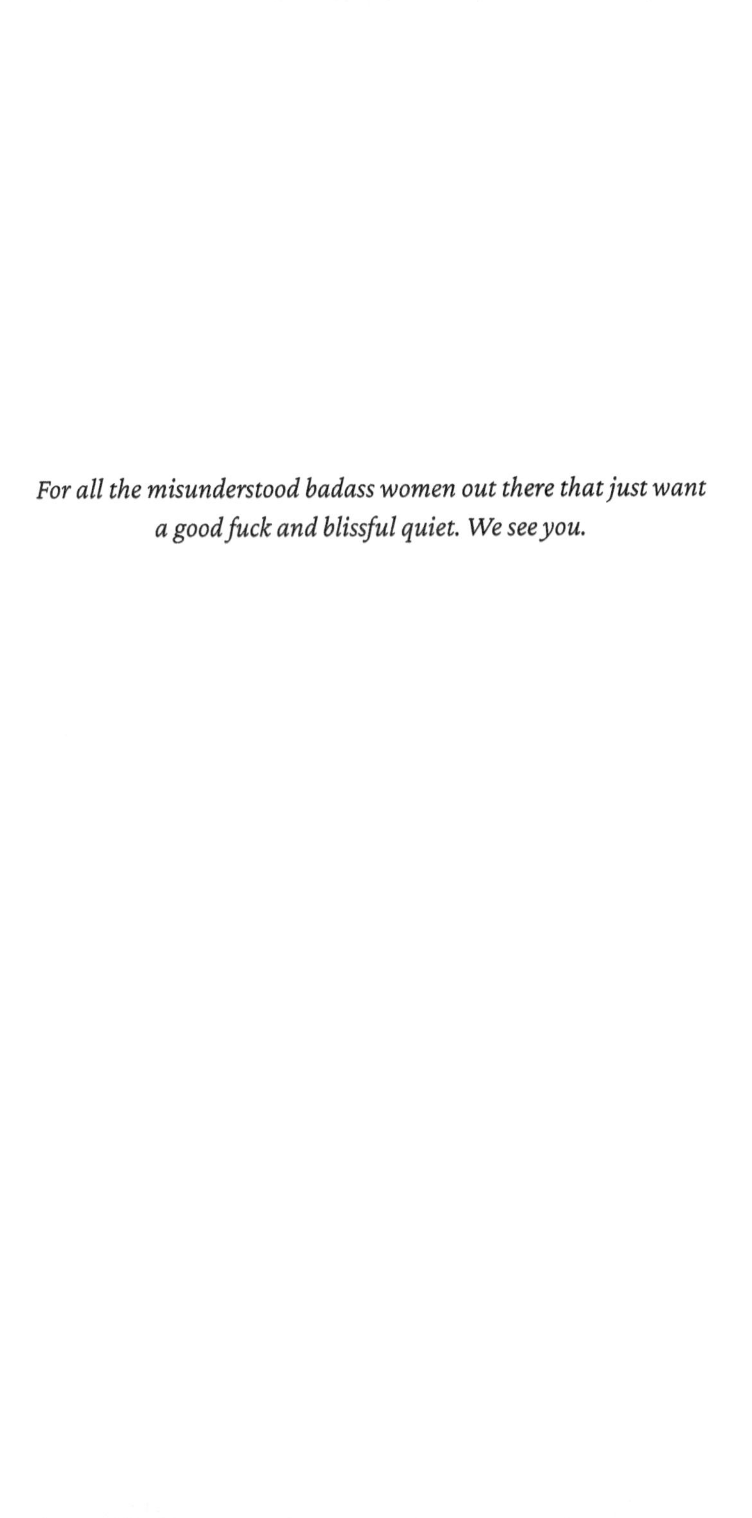

For all the misunderstood badass women out there that just want a good fuck and blissful quiet. We see you.

CHAPTER I
PAN

Nightmares plagued me. Awake or asleep, it didn't matter.

Her ghost lingered. Phantom touches caressed my skin. Peals of her laughter echoed, and whispers of shattered promises replayed in my mind. The scent of her arousal and the memory of her heat against my body toyed with my sanity.

Gods, I missed her, or at least that version of her.

"Fuck," I growled, running my hands through my hair. It felt like an eternity since I'd heard my own voice, and even then, it was only to scream. Sitting up from my bed, I shook off the madness as it tried to sink its claws into me.

She wasn't here. No one was.

My steps were silent as I crossed the room. The eerie glow of candlelight flickered, casting a shadow dance on the walls of my underground tomb. I stopped at her altar. An altar made not for what she was to our realm, but for what she had once been to me. All that remained was a single black feather. An iridescent shade of dark blue shimmered when brought near the light.

I smashed my fist into the marble dais.

I would not mourn for what could have been. I knew what that led to. Pain. Death. Destruction. It was all her doing, and there was nothing I could do to stop it . . . nothing except what I was doing now.

"Your Majesty?" A voice broke through my thoughts, and I turned to see a young shifter standing at the bottom of the stone steps that led to my quarters. His lower half resembled a goat, and his upper remained human-like. A faun? In Arcadia?

"What's happened to you, child?" I asked him, my voice scratchy from years of disuse in my solitude.

The boy dipped his head, casting his eyes down. "One day I tried to shift when I was playing with my sister, and I've been this way since," he said quietly. "Our power . . . it's like we're broken."

"What do you mean by that?" The child was stuck mid-shift, and my brows furrowed as concern lanced through me. "You said 'our' . . ."

Refusing to meet my gaze, the boy continued. "It's what's happened to us all."

My heart sank.

Had this truly happened to all of Arcadia? I'd tried to protect my people. Instead, I'd damned them.

"The guardians sent you for me, haven't they?" I glanced at the parcel he held in his hands.

He nodded. "I come with a message from the Temple of the Gods," he said softly. I approached him, taking the parchment and unrolling it. Tufts of wolf fur had been placed inside, one brown and one gray—and now they were speckled white.

The demand was simple.

It is time.

My hands shook with fury, and I crumpled the paper as I headed to meet them. I ascended the stairs that led from my tomb to the world above.

Arcadia.

My home.

How long had it been since I'd breathed fresh air? Smelled the night irises? Run through the forests?

Too long.

I climbed and climbed.

When the first light of day reached me, my steps quickened. It was only when I saw a figure standing in front of the entrance that I slowed to a stop. A tall, slender woman in blue robes regarded me with cold eyes.

"Go back to your temple, priestess. You're not welcome here." My voice came out thick. Dark.

She raised a single brow. "Have you decided to end your self-imposed exile, my king?" At that moment, she glanced behind me. I turned to see the faun-like boy as he approached from his climb up the stairs. The sadness in his expression tore at me. "You see what you've done to your people? They looked to you, and you abandoned them. You are no god." She curled her lip in disgust.

I ground my teeth together, canines lengthening.

My love for my people was unending. Arcadia had once been a paradise with thriving cities and happy shifters. That had changed over time as one catastrophe after another ravaged our world. I didn't want them to suffer any more than they already had, and even in my attempt to protect everyone, I'd continued to harm them.

"And you are no guardian, priestess."

Her eyes narrowed. "This is your fault, Pan. You have failed to uphold your duty, and Arcadia suffers the consequences of your actions. *You* have done this to your people. You have turned them into perverted versions of themselves. Not us."

My gut twisted. "Give me Flora and Fauna. They're a part of my soul. You trapped them, and I want them back." And they were aging. Their fur . . . the flecks of white. If they died, I would dive straight into madness. A part of me knew I was already headed there.

The corner of the woman's lips twitched. "The terms are the same as they've always been, since the very first day you walked yourself to this tomb. You're welcome to retrieve them anytime you like. . ." She let it trail away, the meaning flashing in the dark depths of her eyes.

"So long as I bring you Kali," I finished.

She nodded.

My hands clenched and unclenched.

I knew the bargain, but for the first time in my incredibly long existence, I'd chosen to go against it. My soul had paid the price, and I could live with that. But the faun boy . . . my people? Arcadia had fallen. To see what would become of them . . . that I couldn't bear.

"Bring her back to us, Pan. We're her guardians, and she belongs here."

"Guardians?" I scoffed, seething at the notion this woman was maternal in any way. "You're fanatics. Nothing more."

"You have no say in her destiny, god of shifters," she countered with equal derision, the pitch of her voice rising with each word. "Get back in your place, and do what is expected of you," she looked at the faun boy and pointed, "or your people will descend into madness with you."

I hated it.

Hated the priestesses.

Hated the choices I was given.

Pressing my lips together, I dipped my chin once.

The priestess smirked. "The sand falls in the hourglass, my king."

I watched her walk away, wanting nothing more than to stab my dagger into her spine. But it would do no good.

The young child stayed by my side, looking up at me.

I dropped to one knee, meeting him at eye level. "Say nothing of this, do you understand?" I said quietly, and he nodded. "Good. Go home to your family." I ruffled his hair and sent him on his way.

I was three steps away from leaving my tomb. A prison of my own making. If I left, there would be no going back. All of Arcadia would know I had returned. And all of Arcadia would assume why.

The priestesses' words echoed in my mind.

It is time.

I felt a change in the forest the moment I stepped over the threshold. My people. A current sizzled in the air, the powers of all shifters connecting and reuniting with their god. They felt me, just as I felt them.

I could hear their laughter. Their prayers. Their hope.

I felt their love, their desire, and their thirst . . . just as I could feel their bitterness, their sorrow, and their rage.

Animals shrieked in the distance. A wild call to our inner beasts. Their king had emerged.

It was time.

CHAPTER 2

ADORA

WHY IS IT THAT ALL REALLY GOOD DREAMS ALWAYS END BEFORE you get to the best part?

Usually my dreams were weird and vague—at least those parts that I'd remember. It was rare that I'd remember everything. Sometimes I'd get a real nightmare about losing my family or the massacre that killed my biological parents. It wasn't like I actually remembered said massacre. I was a newborn when it happened, but my psyche remembered.

But this dream . . .

This one wasn't like any other.

The land was lush. Warm. Crystal clear water fell from a rocky outcrop high above me. Verdant ferns popped up from cracks along the rockface with some sort of glowing algae. I couldn't see where the waterfall ended up, but the spray touched my legs as my toes curled in wet sand.

As amazing as it was, the tropical paradise wasn't even the best part. That award went to the sexiest man I'd ever seen as he pounded into me with some kind of hip roll, slowly driving me insane.

Dark hair fell around his face, creating a curtain between us and the surrounding paradise. He had bronze skin and wide shoulders. His muscles were significant, but not beefy like so many of the shifters back home. It was said that you can't visualize a face you've never seen before, but his features were plain as day. Yet, I was absolutely certain that I'd never laid eyes on this man. He wasn't the kind you'd forget—and that wasn't just because he fucked me like a god.

"Who owns you?" he grunted, kissing my heated skin. When I didn't answer, he growled, his chest vibrating, the sensation sending shivers up my spine. Vines wrapped around my ankles and knees, spreading me for him. "Who fucking owns you, Kali?"

"Kali?"

That wasn't my name.

What the hell?

The dream evaporated. Instead of the warm sand against my back, and a hot, hard body pressing into mine— I woke in a cold bed. Empty. Alone, as usual. My phone screen lit up my tiny room and it buzzed so hard against the nightstand that it rattled obnoxiously.

Two thuds sounded from the wall beside me, followed by an annoyed voice. "Can you get that?"

I sighed.

Fucking vampire hearing. Not that shifter dorm-mates were any better on that front.

You'd think the walls would be spelled for sound proofing when an assortment of supernaturals lived there, but no. Instead, the walls were paper thin and poorly insulated. They claimed it was because they were destroyed regularly from fighting or fucking, but I thought whoever was in charge of budgeting was just a cheapass when it came to living conditions.

I reached for my phone, already knowing who would be on the other end. Not many people had my personal line. Even fewer would call it at such a late hour.

"What?" I answered.

My sister's voice flooded through the shitty speaker. "Why do you sound like a chain smoker?"

I rubbed the sleep from my eyes and cleared my throat. It did jack shit. "Because it's four in the morning, and not all of us have a filthy rich vampire mate that can portal us around the world for vacation."

"It's not vacation," Elias said.

I couldn't make out my sister's response as Danni squealed. It didn't take much imagination to figure out what they were doing. I groaned. "Seriously, you can't wait until after you're done to call me?"

"Hey," she protested. "We're not—"

"Save it."

"For your information, Elias is working. So this isn't a vacation. A vacation means that there are no kingly duties or contracts to be signed—" Danni's voice turned muffled as the phone shifted. I rolled my eyes. Not having sex, my ass. "Or people requesting an audience with one of us. Nope. This is not vacation. It's just a . . . leisurely tour through all of his properties so that I can get acquainted with all of Blood and Beryl."

"Mhmm." I tried to clear my throat again. "Blood and Beryl. Suuuuure. Whatever you say, sis."

Well, it was true that Blood and Beryl did have many territories and that Danni, who was now queen, needed to become familiar with them.

However, I wasn't an idiot.

She and her vampire mate had been trying to conceive for the better part of the last year and decided that some time away from home—i.e. our moms—was needed. Namely so they could fuck like rabbits without interruption.

Not that it had ever really stopped them before.

Danni wasn't quiet. Even after the soundproofing Elias had installed when one of our moms made an offhand comment about it last Christmas, we could *still* hear her.

Apparently, complete soundproofing wasn't an option because "safety reasons."

I called bullshit on that given the sly smirk Elias made whenever it was mentioned, but what did I know? I was just a peacock shifter, sister of the Queen.

"I'm sorry that I woke you. I didn't mean—I mean—I didn't realize the time difference. It has me all mixed up." I tried really, really hard not to think about the background noise coming through my speaker or why her breath was suddenly so hitched.

I cut her off with a heavy sigh and pinched the bridge of my nose. "It's fine. It's fine. Really. Where are you now?"

"Southeast Asia. It's absolutely beautiful here. I think you'd love it. It's a bit too warm for me, and it's way too humid for Nova. But I think that your peacock would be in heaven here."

I nodded along while she kept talking, then remembered she couldn't see me. I switched to making the appropriate vocal acknowledgments when needed, while desperately wishing I could go back to sleep, or more accurately, back to that dream . . . Except the longer I tried to remember it, the more it slipped away, leaving me feeling uncomfortably hollow.

Portal Watch had its perks, namely the bachelorette (or

bachelor) lifestyle that we all led. It made for some pretty awesome parties almost every night. Sometimes one of the embassies got hold of the good kind of contraband. Faery wine from the world of the fae. Ambrosia from the world of the gods. Every now and then, one of the Watchers would transfer, switching places with one from another Portal Watch location. It was something of an unspoken tradition to bring whatever goods you got from your old post to your new one.

Goods like that also didn't hurt for making acquaintances.

I'd made several friends as a result—and some friends with benefits. I'd always been one to prepare for anything, and that included stockpiling methods of payment . . . or bribery. Tomato, tomahto. So, sure, I came bearing gifts from around the world that I'd acquired during my apprenticeship period. You never knew when you might need it.

But as great as the bachelorette lifestyle was, there were still drawbacks.

Early mornings being the largest one. I wasn't sure whose idea it was to switch shifts in the morning but given that there needed to be people on watch for twenty-four hours a day, seven days a week, all year round, I was convinced that it was one of the *morning people* who were at fault. After all, if you have to do twenty-four-hour shifts, wouldn't it make more sense to do—I don't know—noon to noon? Nine to nine? I mean really, there were a lot of options that didn't involve early morning.

But I digress—mornings were the quietest. There was something bittersweet about watching the sun rise on the Portland skyline. It made my chest feel less heavy, but also pointedly reminded me of the missing piece that just always seemed out of reach. I was good at ignoring it. I did a great job of filling it with empty fucks, shallow relation-ships, and whatever good food I could find.

Danni was leading the life she was meant for. Stable. Steady. Filled with greatness, but still surrounded by people that loved her. Meanwhile, I was living mine to its fullest. Mostly. Sometimes when it was quiet and I couldn't be distracted, that missing piece inside me was painstakingly obvious.

Reminding me that maybe, more than likely, I was meant for something more, and it was just out of reach.

"Adora? Are you listening to me?" Danni's voice snapped me back to the present.

"Yes, sorry. Shit. It's just really early right now. I need to get ready for my shift—"

Danni sighed. "This wasn't just a social call, unfortunately."

"Not you too." I knew what was coming and couldn't help the groan that escaped me as I put the phone on speaker and stripped off my night t-shirt, tossing it on the floor along with my other dirty clothes. "Let me guess, Mom told you to call me?"

Danni sighed, her breath making the speaker crackle. I really needed to replace the piece of crap I called a phone, but the thing was damn near indestructible, a positive in my profession. "Technically Abby told me," Danni said.

"That hardly makes it better, you traitor." I picked up a clean sports bra hanging over the back of the overstuffed armchair that took up a third of my room. The rest of it being a full-size bed, nightstand, and armoire. I didn't mind since I didn't exactly have much stuff to begin with. The armchair really just served as a place to put all of my clean laundry since I was allergic to folding it. Organization wasn't exactly my strong suit.

"Oh, come on. When you said you wanted to join Portal Watch, you promised me you'd visit often, but I haven't seen you in six months." Her accusation stung when I could hear the hurt in her voice. Guilt ate at me.

"I said I'd be home for Christmas."

"You also said you'd be home for Thanksgiving, but that didn't happen."

We weren't exactly a religious family, but our mother believed that holidays—even very antiquated holidays—should be spent together, something she raised us to also believe. I picked a pair of faded black jeans off my armchair of clean laundry and stuck my legs through the holes.

"I know, I know, but there's like a billion holidays and I'm not the only one taking time off. Someone has to guard the portals, ya know? They don't just close for Hanukkah or Diwali or the commemoration of the Great Sacrifice."

"There's also like a billion Watchers. Why can't someone else take one for the team?"

Because I volunteered.

Not that she knew that.

It wasn't that I didn't want to see my family. I loved them more than anything, but I also was trying to figure out some things.

At the end of my training, I got to pick which portal I wanted to be stationed at. Six months had passed since then, and I could argue with myself and ask why I'd chosen to return to Portland, but it was always the same lie. I said it was to stay close to my sister, Dannika. To stay near our moms. The truth was, I'd chosen to return home because some inexplicable thing pulled me to this place with magnetic force.

I couldn't make sense of it.

Maybe I was imagining it.

Maybe I was having grandiose thoughts about who and what I was.

Maybe I was going nuts. It was rumored that peacock shifters often did, not that I would know since I was the last one, so maybe that was just some bullshit people made up.

But whatever the reason, the feeling that something was missing was ever-present. I needed to find it, and it seemed to be tied to the shifter portal into Arcadia.

I traveled all around the world to each of the seven portals during my apprenticeship. I'd seen them. I touched every single one. Hell, I'd even crossed through into the world of fae. My moms would have a conniption if they knew that I'd jumped over into the land of fairy a few dozen times for the wildest fucking nights you could imagine—but none of them called to me the same way that our portal did.

There was just one problem.

Anyone that entered the Arcadian portal never returned. We weren't sure why or how. All we knew is that any shifter or person with shifter blood that crossed over hadn't come back in over twenty years. When other creatures crossed, if they came back right away they were okay, but every time there was an expedition to find out what was going on, the Watchers tasked with that mission never returned.

Eventually people stopped crossing all together. So instead of doing something crazy and reckless like I typically would—such as going through the portal when the shift change was happening—I chose to guard it. To watch it. To listen.

When I put a lot of thought into it, I figured I was probably going crazy since no one else seemed to hear the tempting whispers that came from it. But on the off chance

I wasn't, I didn't want to be away for even a moment in case whatever was calling got tired of waiting.

"I'm still new," I explained, giving my sister the explanation I'd prepared. "I've only been an official Watcher for six months. The newer you are, the less time off you get." It wasn't a lie, even if it wasn't the whole truth.

Danni made a disgruntled noise. "Yeah well, if you back out on Christmas, Mom has threatened to come to the portal *in person*. Abby said this is your warning. No missing Christmas."

I groaned. "I said I would be there."

"Yeah, I know," she said, "but you also said the same thing on *our* birthday, and then instead of coming home, you let me break the news to her. Which was crappy by the way—"

"There was a real emergency!"

"And Thanksgiving wasn't an emergency? You just chose to not come home?" she asked in a very neutral tone, something Danni had picked up from being queen. Damn it. She was getting better at this.

"I didn't say that."

"You're lucky I didn't give in to Mom when you didn't show for Thanksgiving. She'd asked—no, wrong word— she'd damn near demanded that I send an official order from Blood and Beryl stating that Adora Kresley was to be sent back to the capital."

I let out a string of curses as I dug through the laundry on my armchair. "She said that?"

"Yup," she answered, popping the "p."

"Please tell me you reminded her you're a queen and an adult. You don't have to do what she says."

We'd had this conversation. Many, many times before.

"Of course I didn't. Abby did, but she's got a point. So if

you're not here on the 20th—as promised—I'm going to pull rank."

"That's cruel."

"Missing our birthday and making me tell Mom you weren't coming was cruel," Danni replied. "I haven't seen you in ages and I miss you. We all do, even Elias—"

"Okay first, there was a damn dinosaur that came through the portal! A *di-no-saur*, Danni. That was a new and unexpected experience for everyone. You saw the pictures."

"Excuses, excuses."

"Second, don't even go there. Guilt me if you must, but the only person Elias cares about is you, dear sister, which is fine. Good. Fantastic, really. I wouldn't want it any other way. Don't make it weird, though."

"Well if you won't listen to me about that, let me tell you about the guy we met with in New York. He'll be at the Earth and Emerald winter solstice celebration and still needs a date. He's in the supernatural syndicates. An heir to the Brooklyn syndicate, I think. What was his name? Aaron? Ashton? No, that wasn't it. There was an A..."

"Adrian," Elias offered.

"That's it," Danni said. "He was so fine, Adora—"

Elias growled and the phone changed hands after a muffled exchange. I glanced at the clock and hurried through getting dressed the rest of the way. "He is your type," Elias said on speaker. "Pretty boy. Dark hair. Delinquent."

"What?" I asked, looking up from lacing my boots like he could see my face.

"What?"

Now he was just being an ass on purpose. "Why do you say—"

"Because the last guy you brought home was wanted by three different Houses," he said apathetically.

"Only two," I said, getting defensive in tone. "The third wanted him as a hostage for negotiating with the other two."

"The one before that was a man *I* sent you to detain for murder."

"It was justified."

"And the art thief?"

"A victimless crime."

Dannika cackled like a damn witch in the background.

"My point, Adora. Thanks for making it."

For fuck's sake. "It's too early in the morning for your bullshit, your *majesty*. I'm hanging up. Tell Danni I promise I'll be there and tell her to call me later when you're off doing king shit."

Elias snorted as I hit "end call".

Prick.

I stood in my room for a moment, huffing over how my day had started. If early mornings weren't already bad enough . . .

Come to me.

Unease ran through me as that phantom command I'd heard for months made an appearance. It was the same thing every time. The same three words. But it was usually at the portal, never reaching me this far away.

I tossed on my leather jacket and was out the door before I could think much about it. It really was too early for this shit—hearing voices included.

Still, restlessness scraped against my insides. A nervous energy I couldn't push away. My fingernails tapped against my thigh in an unsteady, erratic rhythm. A blustery wind lifted stray hairs away from my neck as I left the Blood and Beryl embassy dorm.

It was winter in Portland. My least favorite season. Cloudy gray skies and freezing temperatures were unabating, dragging the days out until they bled together. It was significantly worse if it rained or snowed. While pretty to look at from the inside, my peacock was not pleased to be outside and *in it*. As we shared a body, I tended to agree.

As I took a quick detour through the commissary, I couldn't avoid overhearing the two Watcher's conversation in front of me as I waited in line to grab a banana and protein bar.

"So there I was, listening to her brag about her travels and how *worldly* she is, while she used different lingo for the countries she was talking about, but I got confused because it was gibberish, and I was like, 'but what's a latterine?'"

"A what now?"

"Right? She looked at me like I was stupid, and it said it's a bathroom."

"Wait, did she mean 'latrine'?"

"Yeah, and I corrected her, but instead of admitting she'd simply mispronounced it, she doubled down and insisted that's how they say it overseas."

A short pause. "Yeah, no. I was stationed abroad. She made that shit up."

"That's what I said, but when I called her out on it publicly, suddenly *I* was the asshole."

I sighed as they broke out in laughter, leaning my head back and closing my eyes.

Come to me.

Jesus, it was bad today. Worse than it had ever been. A small part of me hoped that meant my waiting was almost over. The rest of me was side eyeing the fuck out of myself. What "wait"? I didn't even know.

"Next," the attendant barked.

I moved forward and flashed him my food order so he could mark it down for inventory. I took the long way down to the portal, avoiding the cold for as long as possible. When I touched ground level, I braced myself as I stepped outside.

Taunting whispers rode the wind. *Come to me.*

I blinked slowly, eyes opening.

This was new. The voice was distinctly masculine, both smooth and tempting. I knew it had been just a few weeks since I'd been laid, and that dream was something else, so surely I wasn't having withdrawal to the point of hallucinating. A girl knew how to take care of herself, if you know what I mean. But still . . . I shook my head and glanced at the portal once more, staring into the swirling blue and green depths.

Thirty feet in diameter, the Arcadian portal loomed over most everything. Around it, scaffolding had been built to form the bridge—four levels of security that the Portal Watch occupied.

I typically served on the first floor. The main one.

It was the closest to the portal and made direct contact with anything and everything that came through, which meant I got to fight on the front lines.

Not that there was ever much action.

A few dozen animals. Occasionally a shifter in partial shift. I hated those. They came through so disoriented, they couldn't finish shifting one way or another and they'd end up dying in a few days.

That dinosaur a month ago was the most fun I'd had in a while. Not every day you got to fight a giant bird-lizard.

Very little provided a reprieve from my endless waiting for something. What that something was, I didn't know. It was hard to explain.

I just felt it. That pull. And I didn't dare tell anyone.

Maybe it would be good for me to leave for a couple weeks. Clear my head. People joke about going crazy, but I was really starting to question it.

As if it heard the direction my thoughts had gone, that mysterious voice whispered once more.

Come to me.

Those honeyed words were all too appealing. I was tempted to cross. I almost had, once. It was when I had volunteered to stay behind again, not going home to visit my family. The desire to see my sister was ever-present, even if I was the one keeping myself from taking leave.

In some ways, I just convinced myself that my duty was to the Portal Watch, and Danni's was to our House, Blood and Beryl.

That didn't make it any easier.

I'd left my family and all I'd ever known behind to travel the world.

Because of a fucking feeling.

A sense of longing I didn't understand. When I found nothing, I'd come back here searching for the unknown. Waiting. Watching.

And nothing. I pinched the bridge of my nose, squeezing my eyes shut.

Come to me, the portal whispered louder, as though it were near me.

My eyes shot open. Okay, that wasn't a voice in my head. It had come *from* the portal. I drew closer, slowly. I'd never stepped over the line. I wanted to.

Gods, I wanted to.

The prospect of never returning . . . prospect nothing. The inevitability of it . . .

It was one thing to leave my family.

Another to *leave* them.

I stepped closer, my face only inches away from the swirling magic that connected our world to Arcadia, and that invisible pull in my chest tightened.

A hawk shifter called down, "You sure you want to do that?"

"I'm just looking, June," I said, my voice quiet as uneasiness set in. In the multi-colored depths, I saw a face.

Eyes.

I squinted, leaning in to examine it.

"You're clearly forgetting that giant-ass dinosaur we had come through—"

June's voice cut off as a hand came reaching through the portal.

If you will not come, you leave me no choice.

I jumped back in surprise, barely escaping the grasping claws by an inch. My heart thumped against my chest, the sound throbbing in my ears.

"What in the actual fuck is happening?" I muttered.

A tattooed arm emerged, followed by a broad chest with strong, powerful shoulders. I took another step back, peering up at the man that came through.

My brain battled with my choice of words. He wasn't just a man.

It was *him.*

The one from my dream that looked like a god. My dream didn't do him justice.

Logic argued that this wasn't the portal to the realm of the gods . . . but that didn't mean other worlds didn't have them. This *being* stood nearly seven feet tall, with green, glowing eyes and cheekbones sharp enough to cut.

If he was a shifter, I'd never encountered anything like him before.

The silence that pulsed around us ended when the sirens went off. Sharp, piercing alarms screamed for backup.

As supernaturals jumped down from the higher levels of the bridge onto the main platform, I kept my focus on him, and it didn't escape my notice that he didn't bother looking in their direction. Not once.

Those verdant eyes stared at me, and only me.

"I gave you the opportunity to choose." Dark hair hung around his face in thick, uneven strands; the portal at his back casting him in shadow.

I'd thought the voice had been a product of my own mind. Being crazy seemed far more likely than what was actually happening. "You were calling me . . ." Part statement, part question; I was at a loss for words.

"I'm the only one that can." His words were deep and husky, but also haunted. I got the distinct impression he was bothered by the admission.

Before I could ask what he meant, my fellow Watchers approached.

"Back away, shifter," Gadric—a pompous warlock with more power than sense—commanded. I barely stifled the eye roll that begged to occur every time he spoke.

The god-man tore his eyes away from me, and annoyance flitted across his features. He sent one look at Gadric, and the warlock suddenly exploded in a cloud of feathers. A cobra chicken stood in his place.

Most people called them Canada geese, but I knew them for what they really were, the feathery devils.

What he'd just done to Gadric was unheard of, and I studied the off-worlder with greater interest. If I had been invested in my job, I'd have attempted to apprehend him like the others around me, but I had the feeling it wouldn't matter. One of the other Watchers jumped forward. Without fail, before they got within feet of the man, they each shifted. *Even those who were not shifters.*

A veritable zoo began to form around us, but instead of reacting to being turned, they didn't attack. They weren't feral. They stopped—then *bowed.*

Clothes and weapons fell to the floor as more changed. One by one, the bridge was whittled down to just me and him.

A cold wind whipped between us, forcing a shiver through me.

Wise, ancient eyes stared back. While beautiful, there was also great sorrow and a savageness there. The dichotomy made it hard to look away from him. His very presence called to me, demanding my attention—but there was no way I planned on telling him that.

It took a few moments before I found my voice. "That was impressive. Also a good choice for Gadric. He's probably better off this way, but I can't say I've seen that trick before." I gestured at the animal pack around us. "Who are you?"

"Pan," he answered. "I am the god-king of Arcadia."

The pull. The voices. The indescribable feeling clawing at me. It was him? It never once occurred to me that it was a man calling me. Certainly not the man from my dream. I'd thought . . . well, I'd thought it was destiny or some shit, as cheesy as that sounded. Or that I was a step away from losing my mind.

There was a reason I'd never told a soul.

"God-king," I mused, flicking my ombre blue braid over my shoulder. "That sounds important."

His face didn't crack, and even though he tried to hide it, I saw amusement in the quirk of his mouth. "Do you have a point to make before we return to Arcadia?"

Return?

I'd never been to Arcadia before . . . no one had.

"For someone who is so *important*," I paused, letting my eyes travel the length of him in an assessing manner while suppressing the desire to lick my lips, "why are you here, for me, specifically?" I pushed my power toward him. That power that caused the massacre of my kind. The one that could drive a person crazy.

The *Eyes of God*.

I wanted to know what I would see in his soul. What kind of man was standing before me, and what his intentions had been in his past. What kind of person had just crossed through this portal?

My powers could tell me a lot. All I had to do was choose to look.

Nothing happened.

All I found was . . . a wall. A dark wall blocking my access. I occasionally had trouble reaching someone, especially if they were good with shield magic, but it was rare to see absolutely nothing.

Pan regarded me closely with tight eyes and flared nostrils, and I felt a prickling sensation along my spine, like he knew I'd just been trying to pry into the depths of his very being.

That was impossible.

No one knew I was a peacock shifter, and no one knew I held those powers.

My entire life, my family and I kept my secret hidden

from everyone because it was safer to be considered a useless, broken shifter than a peacock. Most people didn't ask what kind of shifter I was, but the few I'd been forced to answer thought I was an abused wolf. One that was horribly mutilated, and therefore didn't shift, but was really good at fighting and had a smart sense about people. After-all, who better to fight and not give a solitary fuck than someone who had nothing to lose?

So how could this newcomer have an idea of what I was just trying to do?

"I'm here to bring you home."

"Home?" I repeated slowly in disbelief. "To Arcadia?" His eyes narrowed, and while he didn't answer, that was answer enough.

I considered his words. I could go. I could also turn around and leave. Though something told me the god-king would have something to say about that.

Truthfully, I didn't want to walk away from this.

Part of me always knew I'd walk through that portal, but I couldn't stand the guilt of knowing I may not return. Hesitation made me complacent for six months. I didn't want to spend more of my life stuck in a liminal state while trying to find my purpose.

I was the only one of my kind that survived that night. My mom—Danni's mom—found me untouched beside the body of her fallen mate. There wasn't a scratch on me, nor was there a peacock shifter nearby. She had no idea where I'd come from, only that her first mate, Scott, had protected me.

It soon came to light that I was the last. All other peacocks had died that night.

There had to be a reason—more to the story than what my either of my moms knew. I wanted answers. I knew deep in my bones there was more to my existence, but crossing that threshold meant there was a possibility I'd never see my family again. My chest tightened at the thought of leaving them forever.

I'd just promised Danni . . .

Running my tongue over my teeth, I took a deep breath. "I need to talk to my family first."

"That's where I'm taking you," Pan said.

My pulse quickened. "What? I have family there? There are more peacocks?"

He extended a clawed hand, but not as forcefully as I would have expected. Even though he had some sort of commanding alphahole presence he exuded, Pan seemed cautious around me. "Are we doing this the easy way or the hard way, *Kali*?"

My body jerked.

It was like a bolt of lightning struck me.

I'd heard that name before from his lips, in my dream. That was crazy, though. Or was it?

I could see into a person's soul and know every secret.

Maybe this was another power the peacocks had, but no one knew? Maybe it was a vision of what I was in the future? In which case, he'd eventually fuck me into oblivion —not sad about that—but he'd also be calling me by another woman's name—which wasn't cool.

I could handle role play, but I didn't fancy being called something else. "That's not my name."

"What I call you does not matter."

My eyebrows lifted sardonically, and I put my hands on my hips. "Then you won't care if I refer to you as *Entitled One*—"

"Hard way it is."

Pan wrapped his fingers around my neck, and before I

could protest, my senses went wild. The moment our skin made contact, a jolt of electricity shot through me. My blood turned to molten lava at the barest touch of his skin, sending a buzzing sensation all over my body.

A feral spark flashed in his eyes. Pan smirked as he pulled me into his world—a world of dark magic and chaos.

A world of beasts.

CHAPTER 3

PAN

E_NTERING_ A_RCADIA_ _WAS LIKE BREATHING FOR THE FIRST TIME._

My chest expanded as magic filled my lungs. I'd only been on Earth for a brief moment, but it was long enough to starve my senses.

The damp air and scents of home enveloped me. I would have found peace in it, were it not for *her*.

I dropped my fingers from the base of the peacock shifter's throat. Her touch burned enough to cause me pain, but not enough to deter me from doing it again. Pain was at least something. A feeling. It had been a long time since I felt anything outside of madness.

"Gods," she groaned, squeezing her eyes shut. The sound made my cock twitch, and I turned away. "The air is water," the peacock choked. "And it's so hot—"

"It's Arcadia," I replied. "What did you expect?"

The tropical-looking trees grew hundreds of feet tall, their wide heart-shaped leaves blotting out most of the night sky. Phosphorescent butterflies that danced in the dark lit the forest floor. A rainbow of colors and hues lined our path.

"Hot, rugged, shirtless men," she deadpanned. "Preferably with tattoos and excellent knot-tying skills."

I glanced over my shoulder to lift an eyebrow in her direction. That was a mistake.

The blade she pressed to my throat proved just how much I'd underestimated this strange creature. Determination made her brows furrow. Sweat dotted her temples. Blown pupils and her bottom lip trembling *just* enough to see made her a glorious and deadly sight.

I'd seen it a hundred times before.

Though never so fragile and unsure as this.

The novelty of it made me smirk, leaning into the metal's sharp edge.

"What do you plan to do now?" I asked. "Cut me?"

She half shrugged, not lowering the blade a fraction. "Depends. You're a god, so I don't imagine it's that easy to kill you." She imagined correctly, not that I would tell her as much. "Then again, getting cut to pieces isn't fun for anyone. Well, unless you're doing the cutting."

This was familiar. Her ruthless irreverence. As if she were talking about the weather instead of murder.

Gold dribbled down the handle.

I hadn't realized she cut me until the evidence was touching her fingers. Flashes of a past I couldn't forget assaulted me.

Knives to my throat. Cunt wrapped around my cock. Nails scratching down my chest.

We'd fucked hard as we fought.

The daydream vanished when she spoke. "You said you were taking me to my family." Her voice quivered—barely, but it was there. *Vulnerability*. She might be the same, but she was also different. "What did you mean by that?"

I sighed, leaning back from the blade.

She was going to ask questions. It was inevitable. I'd barely figured out how to answer them when I'd found her. "You're from Arcadia. Your family is here—"

"I've never been here," she challenged. "Not once. I was born on Earth."

Of course she was. I'd felt it the day she returned.

I always did.

This was the first time that feeling was merely an echo of feeling. A far cry from every past life. She hadn't been here in Arcadia, but she was still back all the same.

"Your blood is from this realm. Your magic. There is family here, your family, and they've been looking for you ever since they lost you." It was the truth. Every. Single. Word.

Her eyes narrowed mistrustfully, but I could see it. The wheels turning. The temptation.

She wanted to *belong*. She always had.

"Why didn't they come for me if they knew I existed?"

"They couldn't," I said. "Earth is no friend to peacocks."

Her lips pressed together. She didn't disagree. There had been a Great Sacrifice on Earth twenty-four years ago. I knew of it. She was born shortly after the battle where her kind were slaughtered. She'd likely been raised either by some unknowing people or wild creatures, though I wasn't sure which to believe just yet.

"And you?" Her head cocked. "How did *you* know where I was?"

I laughed, pressing against the weapon's edge. My blood ran freely, without care. "Darling, I am a *god*. I can easily find a measly peacock shifter."

Righteous fire ignited in her brown eyes, hints of gold flashing in their depths.

Her knife pulled away, and disappointment licked my

skin. The tiny cut healed shut before she lowered the blade to her side. "Which brings us back to my original point, oh Entitled One. Why would you, 'a god-king'," she repeated, using her fingers to make quotation marks in derision, "humble yourself to look for a 'measly peacock shifter'?"

"Because it's my duty," I uttered in all seriousness.

Dubious eyes stared at me, trying and failing to look inside the gaping void of my soul. I knew her powers. "It won't work," I said, calling her out on it. She didn't shrink or blush with embarrassment.

"It was worth a shot." She sighed, looking toward the forest. I could only imagine what she saw. I knew of Earth, but I'd spent no more than minutes there. The damage humans had done to the world was atrocious, and the concrete cities grated on my senses. It wasn't a world for me.

A wicked thought crossed my mind, one I shouldn't have given into, but I couldn't resist. I had to see how she responded . . .

Moving faster than she could track, I grabbed her hand that held the knife and broke her grip. The blade slipped through her fingers, hitting the dead leaves with a dull thud. Then I used my hold to spin her around, so her back was pressed to my chest with my arm braced across her upper body. Using my other hand, I reached between us to snatch her opposite hand and pull it behind her back, causing her top half to push into the arm across her chest while her ass leaned back into me.

My fingers were hard enough to bruise.

"Word to the wise, peacock. Never threaten a god in their own realm."

Instead of fear, the scent of arousal reached me. The wildness in me howled.

"First, my name is Adora. Ah-door-uh. Say it with me."

"No."

She twisted her neck to look up at me from over her shoulder. "For a 'god-king' that takes his duty so seriously, you're rude."

I blinked. "Fine. Adora."

She smiled. While beautiful, it was also wicked. "Second, don't threaten me with a good time."

Her ass thrust back, purposely brushing over my half-hard length. I went rigid as stone instantly. I lowered my head to put my lips at the hollow of her ear. "Do. Not. Ever. Do. That. Again."

She lifted an eyebrow, perhaps testing if I was joking. I wasn't. Upon realizing that, she rolled her eyes and straightened up. Just when I was going to let her go, she stomped down on my right foot. My breath hissed between my teeth. Adora threw her head back, breaking my nose.

I cursed, shoving her forward as she tried to kick me in the knee.

She fell and the vines encircling the tree wrapped around her ankles to form shackles, holding her in place as I reset my nose.

"Hey! How'd you do that?"

"God, remember?" I grunted.

"As if I could forget," she replied scathingly. "Word to the wise, Entitled One. It's an asshole move to feel a girl up and then gaslight her when she gives you the go-ahead."

I growled.

This fucking woman.

Shaking my head, I turned away, taking a moment to gather myself.

Three days if we made good timing, four if not. That's all I had to endure. Then I'd have Flora and Fauna back, my soul's twin animals. Without them, I'd been losing my mind. If they died, I would truly go mad—and the call of the wild that enslaved my people would be permanent.

"The journey to Atlantis isn't far. That's where your family is. If everyone can simply keep to themselves, then we won't have an issue."

"Right. *Atlantis*. That makes sense."

The tone of her voice filled me with exasperation. It was the last thing I needed when I'd be handing her over to them soon enough.

"Is there a prob—" I broke off at the sound of ripping. "What the fuck are you doing?"

Now naked, she sat on the forest floor hacking at her clothes with her knife. "It was freezing in Portland and it's like a sauna here. I'm not going anywhere dressed in jeans and long sleeves."

"How'd you get out of the vines?" One quick look told me she hadn't cut them.

With a mischievous glint in her eyes, she said, "Shifter, remember?"

Warm golden-brown skin acted as the flame. I was the moth.

I swallowed harder than expected and walked away.

We couldn't do this. *I* couldn't do this. Not again.

She'd tried to seduce me before. Was it possible she knew more than she was letting on? That she remembered? I couldn't be sure how much she retained from her past because I'd never known her like this—

"I'm ready."

In a very rehearsed manner, I appraised the newly cutoff jean shorts and makeshift tank top. The sleeves, she'd used to create fingerless gloves. It was smart given the rough terrain we would cross.

She tapped away on a small electronic device.

"That won't work here."

She looked up, closing the device. "Obviously." With a wistful look, she walked toward the portal and tossed it through.

Adora must have read the confusion on my face.

"I left letters. While I wasn't sure when it would happen, I knew I would cross, eventually. Anyway, my sister won't stop looking for me. She'd send our entire House through that portal to wage war if she thought I was kidnapped."

"Your House?"

"It's like a pack, only larger. Houses can have multiple packs, and it's how we govern—that's not important. The point is, I left a message on my phone, so she knows I'm okay. Assuming it makes it back through, she'll find it." Her lips pressed together; eyes tight around the corners.

"I didn't know you have a sister," I said.

She shrugged. "That's surprising. You act like you know everything."

I wasn't sure what to say.

What I did know was this version of her wasn't feral or unhinged. She was *attached*. Loved. Accepted.

Somehow that seemed worse.

CHAPTER 4
ADORA

MY FEET ACHED. SWEAT DRIPPED DOWN MY CHEST, RUNNING IN rivulets over my cleavage. Had I known where I was going or what exactly I'd be doing, I would have packed a bag with snacks, water, and rope.

The latter was good for any number of things.

Traps. Suffocation. Climbing. Sex . . .

My dream came to mind, much as I tried to push it away. I ran my tongue along the edge of my teeth, swallowing down the humid air.

The god-king walked ahead, giving me an unobstructed view of his taut ass in leather pants. How he managed to wear them in this sort of heat confounded me. Probably another god power, if I had to guess. He didn't seem to break a sweat even after hours of walking. The thin white shirt clung to the generous muscle around his shoulders but wasn't damp or sticky. Unlike me.

His wild, dark hair was pulled back from his face and tied with a strip of leather. Symbols peeked out of the collar of his shirt, but I couldn't make them out.

Pan was a curiosity I would have had no qualms about

taking to bed, but the arrogant asshole liked to tease and then turned me down.

I could take no for an answer. I neither cared enough nor was so insecure as to let it bother me.

It was the *reason* that weighed on me.

He hadn't simply refused. He'd reacted vehemently.

Aggressive to the point that it was irrational.

Either Pan had a few screws loose or there was more going on here than he was telling me. I had a nagging suspicion it was somewhere in the middle.

The god-king had the odd habit of jerking his head in various directions every few minutes. His eyes moved as if following the path of something I couldn't see. He clenched his fists when it happened again. My eyebrows furrowed.

"Hey dude, are you sure you're good to take me to my fam—" I started, speeding up to close the gap between us.

Pan twitched, startling far too easy for a supposed god.

The tree nearest us let out a sickening crack. I spun around, trying to gauge which way it broke when the trunk snapped diagonally and fell. I froze.

I could take down a dinosaur without fear, but apparently my quick instincts didn't extend to jumping out of the way from being crushed to death. In the split half-second between when it cracked and then fell, a strong arm grabbed my waist—forcibly moving me.

My head bounced off a hard chest, scrambling my senses. Cinnamon, cloves, and a distinctly male musk fell over me as the forest quieted once more.

Heart pounding and body slick with sweat, déjà vu hit me like a train.

I'd smelled this before. Felt these arms. Heard this heartbeat, as it pounded steady and strong in my ears—like a bass to music only I could hear.

But that wasn't right.

It couldn't be . . . *could it?*

I twisted in his arms. My hands fell on his chest, fisting the lightweight fabric. I used it to hold him to me, close where I could see every facial tic and slight inhale.

"What aren't you telling me?" I demanded.

His pupils dilated. "We need to keep moving."

Or maybe it was like the dream, and this was some vision of the future. Although, it was hard to see that when he was such an ass.

I bit the inside of my cheek, tasting blood. "No. I'm not going anywhere until you tell me what is actually going on. You're being weird. Twitchy. Either there's more to the story or you're on drugs."

His expression didn't change, but I only took that as greater confirmation that I was right.

"How much do you know about me?"

I frowned. "Are you really that much of a narcissist to make this about—"

He leveled me with a cold, flat look. His hands locked around my wrists, squeezing until my fingers went numb enough he could extricate himself. "You wanted to know why I'm 'being weird.' There's no need to insult me."

I pursed my lips petulantly. "Fine. You're a god and a king, obviously. There's no account of you ever leaving Arcadia and coming to Earth. Given that all the shifters that go through the portal have disappeared, most people assume you're not a fan of Earth."

"I'm not."

I snorted. "Other than that, all I know is you're revered as *the* shifter god. Whatever that actually means."

"I'm not the only shifter god," he interjected. "But that's

beside the point. I'm the god of Arcadia and the wild—and *madness*."

My lips parted. "Does that mean that *you're* mad? Or that you make people around you go insane?"

Something uneasy raced along my spine, and it wasn't the sweat. I didn't feel crazy. Then again, did anyone who was actually feel that way? How would I know?

Gods. If Danni knew I'd gone into a portal with this joker—

"Kali! Kali!"

A hail of voices called out, waving their arms in excitement. A couple hundred yards off, people began approaching us. I couldn't understand what they were saying, beyond *that* name.

"Um. Are they real?" I jutted my chin toward the group approaching from behind Pan. He turned his cheek. A muscle twitched there, and I felt it like a warm breath against my skin.

"Unfortunately."

Well, at least I wasn't insane.

I glanced back at the fallen tree to make sure it was there, needing reassurance after Pan's little admission. That he left that out in his whole speech about taking me to my family made me feel unsettled. This conversation wasn't over.

"Not a fan of your loyal subjects?"

"Something like that." I was being a smartass when I asked, but his response made me take a second look at the shifters approaching.

Two larger men walked hand in hand. The taller one was slight in build with a beard that had seen better days. Black, velvety ears stuck out from a mane of salt-and-pepper hair. The shorter of the two had more muscle on him. A black-and-white striped tail flicked in and out from the back of his pants. On his shoulders, a half-shifted child sat with a pointed black nose and large raccoon ears. White fur lightly lined her cheeks, and black rimmed her eyes. Her mouth and hands were human, but her lower half was entirely raccoon.

With them was a single half-shifted woman that I could only make out to be female from her breasts bound in vines. Her face had entirely shifted.

"I'm really not imagining this, right?" I asked. Distaste leaked into my voice, and the god-king visibly flinched.

"No."

"'Kay."

The shifters kept coming toward us, the ones with human mouths smiling and speaking words I couldn't understand. The only thing I could make out was a name.

Kali.

It was the same thing Pan had called me back on Earth at the portal. The same thing he'd said in the dream.

Who the hell was Kali?

"We need to leave." Pan grabbed my wrist, his touch sending tiny shots of electricity through me.

It was that same feeling I'd had for months. The sense of something calling.

If only I knew how to answer.

"They look friendly," I remarked, but didn't stop him from dragging me in a different direction. The raccoon shifters walked faster, breaking out in a run. "Why are we ignoring them?"

Pan growled under his breath. "Because I said we are."

"Oh, of course. How dare I question the almighty Entitled One? Clearly you know best . . ."

He gave me a sharp look over his shoulder. "I'll explain it when we stop for the night."

"Why can't you explain it now?"

I could have sworn I heard him grind his teeth in frustration. "Because I'd rather not have to deal with them."

Behind us, their calls grew louder, more desperate. "Kali! Kali!"

I dug my heels into the ground, bringing us to a temporary halt. Storms brewed behind his gaze. "Don't do this."

His words were a command, but also sounded strangely like a plea. I couldn't decide which it was.

"You called me Kali before." I lifted my chin in defiance. "Now they're calling me Kali."

He cursed. It wasn't in English, yet somehow, I understood it.

That realization terrified me.

I'd only been here a few hours and was already beginning to wonder if maybe this was a mistake.

Maybe some calls shouldn't be answered.

"We don't have time for this."

With that, he bent and grabbed me around the waist, throwing me over his shoulder. My head whipped back before banging into his lower spine. I smacked him with everything I had. It was like hitting stone.

Sexy, warm, fuckable stone—but stone, nonetheless.

One of his arms wrapped around my knees, the other smacked my ass. I got the distinct impression it was not meant to be playful and instead demeaning.

My mouth dropped open in indignation.

All my attempts to knee him or kick were thwarted by his arm keeping me firmly in place while he hauled ass. The raccoon shifters were getting smaller as his speed quickly surpassed theirs. I had to do something.

My side cramped as I twisted, reaching under his arm for my boot. It was easier said than done when my body was shaking like a leaf in a hurricane while he ran, my hips bouncing off his shoulder. It took a few tries, but I managed to catch my boot around the edge. I maneuvered my fingers, straining them to the point of pain as I dug them into the side, grasping for the handle of my blade.

My fingers found purchase right as Pan gritted, "What are you doing?"

I yanked the blade free and stabbed him through the back without a second thought, aiming for his kidney.

Gold blood erupted. Pan dropped like a man kicked in the balls.

My peacock preened.

Served the lying asshole right.

We didn't get long to savor our victory considering he ate a face full of dirt and sent me sprawling. I rolled along the rough forest floor, coming to a stop right as my head smacked into the base of a tree.

Spots of black danced behind my eyes. I groaned.

Shit. Shit. Double shit.

I put a hand to my temple and the other to the ground, trying to will myself to heal faster than a god. Fat chance.

"What is wrong with you?" Pan groaned. His voice sounded close. A little too close. A muffled thump told me he'd just removed my dagger and tossed it out of my reach.

Smart god. Apparently, he did learn.

"You're the one kidnapping me," I snapped.

"You agreed to come through the portal," he thundered. "That's not kidnapping."

"You lied!" I shouted back. Gods, why were we shouting? It was giving me a migraine. Or was that a concussion? Either way, I needed to find out what was actually going on.

"No, I didn't," he scoffed. "Which you'd know if you understood."

"I'd understand if you'd explain," I replied in an aggravated tone.

"You'll understand when we get there and you're reunited with your family."

"Why are you so gods-damned difficult—"

I was cut off by the sound of the raccoon shifters. Their steps slowed as they approached. The black spots faded from my vision, leaving me feeling woozy but cognizant.

"Kali . . . Kaaaali." That name was a cry, a plea, a prayer.

They came toward me, and Pan stepped between us.

I slapped his ankle, trying to sit up.

"Stop," I hissed. "Why are you acting like such a prick?" It was supremely unfair how fast he healed given how high-handed he was being. I should have stabbed him twice before going down.

"You need to run," he said softly.

I frowned, dragging myself into a sitting position. What on earth was he telling me to run from? Him? Because he didn't need to tell me that, I already got there all on my own.

Right as I opened my mouth to tell him as much, the raccoon shifters stopped. One by one their eyes began to bulge. Their teeth grew larger. Their bodies cracked, breaking in places bodies never should.

The child's jaw unhinged, gaping like that of a snake. He let out a feral hiss then climbed down the man's shoulders in a scurry that more closely resembled a spider than a raccoon. The others dropped to all fours, wrists and ankles snapping, making room for larger, more monstrous claws to distend. Fur rippled along their bodies. Back and forth. Back and forth.

They stalked closer, letting out the shrillest of screeches.

It was a call.

I really didn't want to find out what answered.

"Well, shit," I muttered right as they sprang.

Pan met the first two head-on in a clash of talons and fangs, his own body rapidly shifting. I scrambled out from behind him, and army crawled toward where I'd heard the knife drop.

Two of the monster raccoon shifters broke off and started for me. Pan managed to grab the one that had previously been a woman. The child outmaneuvered him with three at his throat.

I tried to haul myself to my feet, thinking I may be better off ditching the blade at this rate.

The thought only lasted a second before something slammed into me from behind and sent me sprawling.

Blackness returned to greet me.

Fucking concussion.

I was starting to think stabbing Pan might have been a poor idea, and what was more, that he may have been right for encouraging me to try to run.

Teeth latched on to my shoulder. Ripping. Tearing.

Pain sharpened my senses and sent a surge of urgency to my brain, clearing the fog long enough to reach back and grab the raccoon–creature–shifter child by the hair. I pulled her off of me, gritting my teeth against the pain as the child ripped out a chunk of me with it.

I flung it forward, trying to get it as far away from me as possible.

The effort sent me back to my knees. One hand hit the ground to steady myself. The other came up to my neck to feel the damage.

Crimson ran like paint, causing another episode of déjà vu to hit.

Gods. I wasn't scared of a little blood, but I wasn't made to sustain heavy bleeding, in a land without healers or hospitals, no less.

A ragged growl drew my attention. The kid was back. Blood dripped from its mouth like a monster out of the *Gremlins* movie from the 80s.

"Don't do this kid," I coughed. "I really don't want to hurt you."

If it could understand me, it gave no indication.

"Pan," I called, taking a step back. My foot hit something hard. My eyes flicked down. Steel glinted in the luminescent hours before dawn. I snatched my blade up without taking my eyes off the kid.

"Little busy here," he said, sounding pissed off to the nth degree.

I bit back the smartass reply ready on my tongue. This was kind of my fault.

"What's wrong with them? Why are they attacking us?"

The raccoon monster took another step toward me, its unhinged jaw opening wide to show a row of very pointy teeth.

My peacock was not impressed.

"Madness," Pan grunted.

"What?"

"They're mad," he snapped, louder. The trees rustled and birds flapped away.

Pitch-black eyes zeroed in on me. I shook my head, hoping that even if he couldn't understand my words, he could grasp what I meant.

"You just said you're the god of madness. Fix them—"

It lunged. I sidestepped, dashing away to avoid a confrontation.

"I can't."

"What?"

"I can't help them." Emotion weighed his words down like lead bricks. I wanted to ask what good a god of madness was if he couldn't fix it, but that wasn't going to help us right now.

"How do I get them to stop?" I asked instead.

"You can't," he answered. A crack echoed. I saw a body drop out of the corner of my eye. The raccoon creatures snarled. "There's no cure save death."

"You can't be serious," I said, continuing to evade my pursuer.

At full strength it wouldn't have been such a difficult task. But after being awake all night, hiking for hours, starving, and fighting off a head injury . . . I'd seen better days.

Another crack sounded. The breaking bones were like a chill running down my spine.

It was one thing to kill for vengeance or in battle, but this . . . they weren't in their right mind . . . and it felt wrong. The same way their malformed bodies were a perversion of what we were, so was killing them.

"Don't you think I'd take it if I had another option?" he said, frustration bleeding through every syllable. "They are *my* people, and my power is corrupting them . . ."

I missed a step, distracted by his admission.

The kid used that moment to close the distance between us. I lifted the knife, hoping to deter it and buy myself time to find another solution.

Hot blood slicked my fingers.

The creature gasped, crimson bubbling up and spilling

out its mouth. I stared in horror as it pulled itself off my blade, then lurched forward again.

Time slowed, and I found myself counting its breaths.

One. Two. Three. Four.

It didn't breathe again.

Slowly the body fell back, sliding off my blade and falling onto the forest floor. Eyes glazed and utterly unhuman, it died like an animal.

My chest tightened.

It was only my months of training with the Portal Watch that kept me grounded in that moment and instead of collapsing into a crying mess. They'd prepared us for every situation they could think of, and that included child soldiers.

It hadn't sat right with me then, and it didn't now.

I lowered my blade to my side, fingers stiff with congealing blood.

Silence fell between us.

He must have killed the third when I was focused on the kid. Pan took a step toward me, and I lifted my chin. "I don't know what you're playing at, but I didn't sign up to kill kids. Either you start explaining *that*," I motioned to the body in front of me, "or I'm out. You may be a god, but I promise you, I will *not* make for a pleasant captive."

Storm clouds and hidden secrets were in his eyes when he looked at me, his expression unreadable.

"I'll tell you what you want to know, but first, I need to give them a proper burial."

I cleaned my blade on my shorts and stowed the weapon in my boot, then crossed my arms over my chest. I nodded. "We'll bury them. But when the sun comes up, I want answers."

CHAPTER 5
PAN

IT'S ALWAYS THE SAME NIGHTMARE.

The skies are red and filled with smoke. Trees are burning. Homes ablaze. Bodies litter the forest floor, a trail of corpses leading up to the white stone archway of Atlantis.

I am running. Racing. Trying to get to her.

The ground trembles and cracks appear. Sand and silt bounce on the surface as the land groans. Deep. Yawning. It sounds like thunder when it splits open. Dirt and debris slide into the cracks, pulled in as the crevices widen and grow.

Wings sprout from my back as I leap into the skies. Lightning forks through the clouds, scorching the air. The better parts of me, Flora and Fauna, morph from wolves to falcons. They flank me on either side, and we battle the wind and rain when it unleashes.

In the distance, across the city where buildings crumble, crack, fall—she stands at the great wall's edge. Her dark blue hair is nearly black from the rain as she faces the open water beyond the city.

On the other side, the ocean churns. Like a sleeping monster awakened, the water begins to circle and pull away from the shore.

No. No.

I beat my wings harder. Faster. Urging myself to reach her in time.

Water rises. A tidal wave forms.

Ten feet. Twenty. Thirty. Forty.

Growing. Expanding. It blots out the last bit of light from the dual suns of Arcadia. Lightning flashes, painting an eerie, haunting scene.

The land shakes and the sea attacks.

"Kali!" I shout, my voice booming.

The figure on the wall turns.

Her electric eyes settle on me.

I can't name the emotion if I try.

The wave hits. The wall breaks. Atlantis capsizes.

My eyes flew open.

The past faded as I stared at the suffocating stone walls. Anxiety filled me, not recognizing them as the sulfur-lined sides of my tomb. Gravel skidding caught my attention. I twisted, shifting my hand to claws.

My breath halted in my chest.

She slept on the slab of rock at the very back of the cave. Her fingers were threaded together behind her head and her dark blue eyebrows were drawn together, the skin between them puckered as if an invisible hand pinched her. Her feet moved restlessly, the hard soles of her boots scraping against the rock and sending tiny pebbles skittering off the edge.

I sighed.

She was the same as she'd always been on the outside, but inside—something was different. Kali never balked at death, be it an elder's or a child's. She certainly never helped give them a proper burial.

Sure, the impatience was there, along with a sharp tongue that no other besides Kali dared have with me. She was built for sin and death. Wild to her very core. But there was also an emotion that I'd never seen in her before in all the years I'd known her: regret.

Adora regretted getting in the way so that the shifters could approach us. She regretted the deaths of those people.

Not for the first time, I wondered if she was this way before I met her.

While every life was different, there were two commonalities that never changed.

The first, that I found her as a baby and didn't see her again until she was a grown woman who'd regained her godhood.

The second was that I killed her.

Sometimes it was difficult, excruciating even, and others, nothing more than numbness. I was able to let it go because what redeeming qualities she'd had—what *we'd* had—had diminished over time. Eventually, her destructive nature had vastly outweighed all else.

Now, I wasn't so sure.

Light disappeared beneath the horizon, bathing the cave in shadows of the past. I shook my head, clearing those thoughts away.

My mission was simple. Find Kali and return her home.

Flora and Fauna would be returned to me. My soul would be restored instead of splintering. I would regain what sanity I lost and put an end to the madness. The call to the wild that drove shifters to become monstrous versions of themselves would end.

That was my job. My duty, as god and king of Arcadia.

So why did I find myself making a distinction between Kali and Adora?

"Are you going to keep watching me sleep like a creep?"

I jolted, no less shocked than if she'd slapped me. "I wasn't watching you."

"Sure you weren't." She opened those mischievous brown eyes, focusing on me instantly. "Are you going to deny being a creeper next?"

I pressed my lips together. 'Creeper' wasn't a term I'd ever heard before, but it didn't take much to get the idea. "We need to get moving. There's only eight hours of night and we need to make up for the delays we ran into yesterday."

Adora arched off the slab, stretching her arms high above her head, drawing her shoulders tight together. A flash of a memory where I had Kali tied up in my tomb while I sucked on the flesh between her thighs made me stifle a groan.

I may have hated her in past lives, but that didn't stop me from taking her to bed in most of them. And there were ones we loved before we hated. Sometimes for years. Decades.

It physically hurt to think of those times when she was here looking at me with those fuck-me lips parted in a seductive smile.

After last time, I swore her off for good. Every life thereafter. We were bound by fate, but the harm she did was too much. Every fuck and affair ended in a catastrophe between us, even though we were continually drawn together like magnets.

But that was Kali, not Adora.

I needed to suffocate the part of me that dared even think that.

"Delays," she mused. "That's an understatement if ever I've heard one. Care to tell me how we ended up here?" She motioned to the cave, dropping her arms and sliding off the rock.

"You passed out during the vigil."

"I must have hit my head harder than I thought." She frowned, taking in her clothes for the first time. "You washed me."

"Washed is a stretch." I jerked my chin toward the mouth of the cave. "There's a small stream that goes down this part of the mountain. It sprays enough off the rocks to get the blood off without too much trouble. Last thing I wanted was you waking up in the middle of the day and getting me up because you couldn't find a shower."

It was a lie. Partially.

I didn't want her waking up. I also couldn't stand seeing blood on her. It made the madness worse.

I'd seen Kali drenched in blood enough for even my infinite lifespan.

"You have showers in Arcadia?"

"Natural ones. Waterfalls. Leaks in caves."

"Not exactly what I'd call a shower."

"Did the lack of steel death traps not tip you off that this isn't Earth?" I lifted my eyebrows.

"You mean cars?" She cocked her head. "Because I'd kill for one of those 'steel death traps' with air conditioning right now."

Of course you would. Because this was Kali. She'd kill for anything, and I shouldn't forget it. "Cars. Machines. Oil rigs. Coal mines. Your planet was trashed in the name of luxury and laziness."

She squinted at me. "I don't see what my planet has to do with anything, but if you're going to go there . . . is this an insecurity thing?" She took a step toward me, her gaze intense. "You lost control of your powers and corrupted your own people, so you have to bag on my home to feel better?"

I took a step toward her. The air between us became charged. Tension, palpable. "You don't get to say *anything* to me about that."

"Really?" she replied. "Because it was *your* powers that caused it, in *your* world, where *you're* in charge, and *you* failed to tell me what would happen." Her voice got quieter with each word as she stepped closer. "I was forced to kill a *child* because of your asinine belief that I should be kept in the dark."

Golden waves rose and fell in the depths of her gaze. A shiver ran up my spine.

I leaned close. "Has it ever occurred to you that I didn't tell you for *your* benefit?"

She snorted. "Horseshit."

My teeth ground together. "You want to be vulgar and disagreeable? Fine. I'll tell you."

She tapped her foot impatiently, hands on hips. "I'm waiting."

My hands balled into fists. I wanted to grab her and shake some sense into her. I couldn't do that, so I settled for second best: feeding her lies dressed as the truth. "Your family took my soul's twin animals, Flora and Fauna. Unlike shifters, who have mates, I have them. They ground me and my power. Twenty-five years ago, your family took them from me. Trapped them using old magic. They refuse to give them back unless I bring you back to them." I had to commend her. Her face didn't show an ounce of emotion as she listened. "In losing them, I've descended into madness, and the entirety of Arcadia with me."

She didn't speak for several seconds. I started to wonder if she would.

"There's just one problem with this little story," she said, voice shrewd. "If this hinged on you finding me, why didn't you?"

Why indeed?

I couldn't give her that truth. No version of it would go over well.

"I'm the god of Arcadia, not Earth. I traveled the entire planet to find you, but *you weren't here.*" A crack appeared in her armor. She wasn't quite sure I was lying now. I was a bastard for laying on the guilt this thick, but I had to. It was the only way. "Arcadia paid the price."

She looked down for a brief moment. "But you called me. Through the portal—"

"I was calling through all the land and portals, trying to draw you closer from whatever world you were in, so that I didn't have to cross over for long and risk my power infecting another population."

The muscle in her cheek tightened. "I see. So because I have a horrible family, apparently I am equally deserving of your scorn. Thanks for clearing that up. We should be going, since I'm guessing I'll need to find breakfast on the way."

She stepped around me and marched toward the front of the cave.

Well, she bought it. Not that it made me feel any better.

Adora was going willingly. This was a good thing. We needed to get through this as quickly and painlessly as possible.

"Are you going to stand there and stare at my glorious ass or lead the way?" she called before rounding the corner.

"I wasn't staring at your ass."

"No, but you *were* staring."

I lifted a brow. "How did you know?"

She paused mid-step.

"I have eyes on the back of my feathers."

A fan of black peacock feathers sprouted from her tiny shorts. It was the first hint of her animal I'd seen, and it was only a slight shift. Not even enough to be called a partial. The onyx feathers swayed.

I could have sworn one winked at me before she disappeared out of sight.

ADORA

"Are we there yet?" I could hear the whine in my voice. Dehydration was going to be the death of me. I knew it. No one could sweat this much and survive. How did peacocks live here? I'd never liked the cold, but this heat was too much—and it wasn't even daylight. Now I'd resorted to whining. A sound that grated my nerves to no end, and I was doing it. I was becoming someone I didn't want to be, and it was all because of the damned humidity in the jungle.

"If you weren't trudging like a petulant child, maybe we'd get there faster," Pan grumbled.

"Excuse me, I am not *trudging*, and I'm not a child," I bit back. "I'm sticky, hungry, and in desperate need of a bath. I'm completely out of my element here with the worst company imaginable—and I spent Christmas with my sister's rejected mate slash former bully at the same dinner table, so that's saying a lot about you. Forgive me if my speed doesn't live up to your unrealistic expectations."

Pan turned to look at me, raising an eyebrow. "I could always throw you over my shoulder again," he suggested.

I rolled my eyes. "Pass. The view isn't worth it."

Pan scoffed, and I grinned to myself. It was a lie, but I wouldn't tell him that. He had a delicious ass, and if he were anyone else, I'd lick the muscled contours of his back with pleasure.

I sighed, tilting my head to the side to ease the cramping. As I did, the damp cloth around my neck wound slipped. It pulled at the freshly healed and still tender skin, and I hissed at the sting.

Pan stopped, leaning over so he could inspect it. He softened as he spoke. "It looks better now. The cave we're headed to has underground springs. Pools. You'll be able to take a proper bath. The sooner we get there . . ." He gave me a look, suggesting I was holding us up.

"Fine, fine. I can't argue with the idea of being clean." I kept quiet, reserving my energy, dreaming of being submerged in water. I had no idea how much time had passed when he started asking questions.

"What did you mean about your sister's rejected mate?" Pan asked, knocking large palm fronds out of the way.

"That you're worse company than him? I figured that was pretty self-explanatory." He side-eyed me while I smirked, but I knew what he was asking. "My sister Danni and I were outcasts growing up. Outcasts get bullied. Sometimes fate is a bitch and mates you to your bully. Fate also allowed her to reject him, thank the gods, but it didn't stop him from ending up in my life. So—"

"You took him as your lover?" he interjected. There was anger in his tone, but also something like jealousy. I couldn't quite place it.

I shook my head. "First—ew. Second—who even talks like that? 'Take him as my lover.' Third, why would you go straight there? I didn't say I *wanted* to spend the holidays with him. I said he still ended up in my life. And also, don't interrupt me. It's rude."

"You weren't getting to the point," he said with a shrug.

"I *was*, actually, but you're impatient." I waited a moment in silence until I knew he wouldn't speak again. "Anyway, Markus—the mate she rejected—he was dating a high-ranking member of our House. So he was with us for the holidays because of her. Thank the gods they ended it and he moved on. I'll tell you what, it was so hard to be near him without strangling him when no one was looking."

"I'm surprised you didn't just kill him."

I huffed in agreement. "I know, right? I thought about it a few times." For a brief second, we were getting along, but when I turned to look at him, there was a hint of sadness on his face. Like somehow my admission showed him something he didn't want to see. I felt exposed, but for the life of me, I couldn't figure out why I cared. It was a new feeling, and I didn't like it. It was all made worse by the fact I couldn't use my power on him. I'd pushed so hard, but all I found was darkness.

"Why didn't you?" he pressed, breaking me from my thoughts.

"Kill him?" I asked, and he dipped his chin in response. I lifted my shoulder. I wasn't sure how much I wanted to share with him. "He didn't actually deserve it. I thought he did at one time, but . . . I don't know. Much as I hate to admit it, he's changed."

He considered me. "I find it curious you're defending his innocence."

I scrunched my face. "What? I never said he was innocent."

"You said he didn't deserve to die."

"Dude, that's not the same. Being guilty of something doesn't mean you deserve death. Motive determines a lot, you know? I don't know what kind of savage system you have here, but so far, I can see why Arcadia doesn't have a thriving tourism industry. The weather is bad enough, but if there's an execution for every wrongdoing . . ." For years, the portal had been off-limits. It made me wonder if all the shifters that passed through had ended up dead. Or gone mad.

Pan tilted his head and hummed, but I had no idea how to read him. "Tell me about your family," he said, that trepidation in his tone leaking through again.

"Danni's dad died the day she was born. When her mom went out to look for him, she found me. I was just a baby at the time, so they didn't know what I was. When no one claimed me, we all just assumed my parents died in the Great Sacrifice. A lot of shifters did. I was just one more orphan of many. Until I shifted into a peacock. By then I was a toddler. My mom took me in—raised me as her own. She's really strong. Not physically, although her wolf is another story, but mentally. She raised me and Danni all on her own until Abby came along. Scott, Danni's dad, was her fated mate. She suffered in ways we didn't see, and then she found Abby. It was only when things got better that we started to understand how much she had been struggling to get by. She kept going for us, but finding Abby made her want to keep going for herself too. Now that Danni is mated and they're trying for a little mutant vampire baby, she and Abby are over the moon to be grandparents. Personally, I think I'm a little young to be an aunt, but no one's asking what I think there, so . . ."

"It sounds like they're important to you," he said softly.

"Uh, yeah. Of course they are. They're my family." Was

this god-king lonely? Did he have a family? Anyone to love or feel close to? Something told me not. What a shit existence that must be. "What about you?" I asked.

Pan instantly bristled—*that* I could read. His whole posture tightened; shoulders tense and body rigid, he cleared his throat. "What about me?"

"Family? Friends? Fuck buddy?" I asked in a casual tone, winking at the last suggestion. "Tell me about your . . . whatever it is you have."

"No." Pan kept his eyes forward, refusing to look at me.

I scoffed loudly. "Why not? I just told you about me."

"It's not your concern."

What. A. Bastard.

"My life isn't your concern either, asshat, but I was nice and told you about some of it. I don't see a reason for the cold shoulder. Maybe you have some psycho ex you don't want to mention. That's fine, but you could at least tell me something. Maybe what it was like for before you 'were driven to madness'?" His dismissive glance told me that wasn't happening anytime soon. Pity. I would have liked to hear about it. "What about how you became a god? Is it immaculate conception like the bible or do you have godly parents? What about siblings? A sister? A twin? A pet goldfish, perhaps?"

As though I hadn't spoken, all he responded with was, "Hurry up. You move slowly."

"You know, you want me to walk faster, talk faster, and stop asking questions. It's really chauvinistic, *oh Entitled One*, the *god of shifters*. By chance, do you also shift into a pig?" I stomped ahead of him, trying to escape his proximity.

"Kali," he called to me.

"I take it back. That's an insult to pigs," I retorted. "Cute creatures, actually. Also turn into bacon, which I like, so they're pretty useful on that front. I've been told they're good for disposing of bodies too." I waved my hands around as I spoke, moving through the trees at a quicker pace.

"*Stop*." The commanding tone did nothing except fuel my irritation with him.

"No, you told me to hurry up." I glanced over my shoulder and yelled, "And it's *Adora*, you giant prick!"

As I marched away, my foot sank into the mud before I started slipping sideways, and I lost my balance, stumbling down onto a slope which—lucky for me—was much steeper than it looked.

I am beauty, I am grace.

Gracefully careening down an embankment while screaming. My leg smacked into a tree trunk as I rolled. Something stabbed into my calf. I came to a stop with a resounding thunk. I was starting to have regrets about crossing the portal. Who was I kidding? We were well past 'starting'.

"I've had about as much of this journey as I can stand," I mumbled, my face pressed into the dirt.

I heard Pan's footsteps approaching from where I'd fallen, and I rolled onto my back. Mud stuck to my cheek. My makeshift clothes were coated in sweat and decorated with detritus from the jungle floor. A throb in my calf forced me to sit up and inspect what had caused the pain.

A thick green thorn was embedded in the muscle. Great.

"Wait, let me help you," he said, kneeling down.

"Go away," I muttered. I yanked the thorn and gritted my teeth at the pain, exhaling through my nose loudly. Slowly, I counted to five while focusing on steadying my breathing. I opened my eyes, cracking my neck and releasing some of the tension in my jaw.

Pan's eyebrows shot up in surprise. "You handled that better than I expected. Those thorns tend to make even the toughest of shifters break down in tears."

"I have a high pain tolerance, but I prefer the kind that requires set up and consent, if you know what I mean. This," I gestured to my bloody leg, "is your fault, so I'm not thrilled."

Leaning back, he glared. "How exactly is this my fault? I told you to stop. You chose not to listen."

"First, you're just being an asshole to me in general, and I have no idea why. I didn't do anything to you. I'm sorry if whatever 'family' I have here treated you badly, but I didn't. *You* came for me, remember?" I pointed my finger at his chest. "Second, my name is Adora. For fuck's sake, no wonder you're alone. If you kept calling her the wrong name, maybe that's why she left you."

Pan's lips pressed together, and he inhaled sharply. Several moments passed before he spoke again. When he did, I cringed.

"She didn't leave me. She died."

Ugh. Fuck my life.

Now I sort of felt bad. He was still acting like a miserable jerk, and I'd taken a shot below the belt. I just didn't think it would land *that* hard.

"I'm sorry to hear that," I said quietly. "I didn't mean to . . ."

"Hurt me?" he suggested.

"No, I meant to jab hard enough to hurt you," I admitted. "Just not like that."

Pan leaned his head back and laughed. It was genuine. Natural. I tilted my head as I watched him, feeling an odd sense of happiness that I couldn't explain. Like it made me feel content to hear his laughter and to see him like this. But I'd known him for all of twenty-four hours, so the logical part of me was confused.

I stood up, brushing my legs off, but that was like sweeping sand in the desert. I was coated, and nothing I could do would make it better. As I looked up at Pan, a soft whistling sound gave me pause.

Weapon, my brain screamed.

I lunged at Pan while he simultaneously wrapped me in his arms, sending us both to the ground right before a spear landed between where we'd been standing. Buzzing all over my body attempted to distract me as I laid on top of him. My breasts pressed into his chest as he held me tight, but adrenaline quickly took over and it was all I felt.

Screaming in the jungle gave away which direction the spear was thrown from.

"Hope it was good for you," I ground out, shoving away from Pan. "We need to get out of here." I had no desire to kill anyone else.

We scrambled to get up, and I felt for my dagger at my boot, pulling it from its sheath. While it wasn't in my nature to run, I was fine doing it if it meant I wouldn't kill another kid.

"Too late," he muttered, scanning the trees. "They're here."

"The same from yesterday? The . . . creatures?"

"Worse."

"What? What do you mean, *worse*?" I whisper-yelled, dagger up and ready. "I haven't gotten a rabbis shot. What's worse than mutant rabid raccoon shifters?"

A crowd of four burst through the trees. Like the day before, some of the shifters were stuck grotesquely mid-shift. In complete contrast, they didn't look happy to see me before things got weird. These shifters looked enraged from the start, like they had a personal vendetta to settle. Like I'd eaten their family dog and used the bones to pick my teeth right in front of them. They looked at me with wild hatred.

And I was ninety-nine percent certain they wanted me dead.

"I come in peace," I shouted, holding my hands out in the universal sign for "stop." Pan snorted.

"Well, they don't," Pan said, in a fighting stance beside me.

"What the hell did I do?" I asked as the first shifter arrived at our clearing, yelling in a language I didn't understand.

They wasted no time lunging straight for us. Pan intercepted two and deflected, tossing one to the side before blocking another attack from a half-shifted puma that appeared to be in charge. The remaining two came at me, and it didn't take long for us to be separated.

Another volley of commands came from the half-puma after Pan managed to toss him, but this time something changed. I didn't know how, but some of the words translated in my thoughts, making sense as if I spoke the language.

Murderer. The One. Attack.

Hearing it tripped me up. A vision flashed in my mind of standing in a forest not unlike the current jungle, speaking to a tribe.

I shook my head, clearing the false memory as a half-wolf turned and lunged for me. I rotated my body, tucking the dagger against my forearm and slashed in an arc, hitting its neck while I ducked and rolled. It landed with a thud, blood pooling around its prone form. I glanced up, seeing Pan cut through a half-bear.

I stayed in my crouched position, frozen, as another scene played out in my mind. Something like another life.

A life where I knew a family of bear shifters, but they weren't stuck in some monstrous in-between. I watched as their cubs changed easily from human to bear with ease while they splashed in a river. A tribe leader handed me a platter—an offering—and there was a look of uneasiness in his eyes...

"Adora, above you," Pan yelled, breaking my trance. I looked up into the tree branches and saw the puma was about to get the drop on me. Panic coursed through my veins.

I sprinted to Pan as the giant cat landed where I'd been moments before. Someone here was playing with my head, but I didn't know who. I'd almost gotten killed because of it, and now I was mad.

"Back-to-back," I shouted. I turned my body, pressing against him and taking a defensive stance as a fox shifter leaped from the bushes snarling, jaws open and ready to bite.

As soon as I saw it, I knew I had only a moment, but I pushed my power into it. I tried to see into its soul. Its mind. Its heart. Anything. No images came through. Just pulsing pain. Anger. Hurt. Generations of sorrow and loss caused by . . . destruction.

And it wanted vengeance.

I let go of my power then threw myself at the fox, forcing it off track using my momentum. It landed with a yelp, and I stabbed into its neck, severing the spine quickly, to minimize the pain. After being immersed that shifter's soul, it felt wrong to kill them, even though they were dead set on killing us first.

I walked over to Pan as he was leaning down, finishing off the puma that had tried to attack me earlier. Wiping my blade on my muddy shorts, I frowned. Not the best way to take care of a weapon, but I didn't have many other options.

When Pan stood, I looked up at him. Some of that pain and sorrow I'd felt from the fox was radiating off their god-king as he stood before me. My sister was the one who'd been filled with an unnatural empathy after her change, but now it felt like it was consuming me too.

As I opened my mouth to tell him I was sorry for the loss of his people, a searing pain ripped through my arm, and I screamed as I twisted around. There'd been five. Shit. Another mountain lion, identical to its dead brethren, had taken a swipe just as Pan pulled me away.

I gripped the wound, and the cat went for me again.

A warm and protective arm pulled me into an unyielding body, holding me close, its hand splayed on my chest just above my breast. I turned to look at Pan, but my vision clouded.

The scenery changed.

Pan held me in the same position, but this hold was tender. His thumb gently stroked my skin. He looked at me with admiration. With . . . love. He looked happy. His eyes were filled with hope. He leaned into the crook of my neck, trailing little kisses to my ear. I could feel the heat of his breath against my skin, and the press of his hardened cock against my backside. I could hear the sound of a waterfall near us, almost drowning out the words he whispered.

You'll were made to be mine.

"Adora!"

Pan shouting and shaking my shoulders brought me back to the jungle. The real world, where we'd just battled a group of half-shifted animals. Where dead bodies littered the forest floor, including my attacker. I came out of my stupor, but the strange memory I'd just seen had me at a loss for words.

I was fully aware of a throbbing pain and blood dripping down my arm, but I didn't much care. I looked at him in a new light while he spoke to me, asking if I was okay. The best I could do was nod.

What had just happened? Could shifters play mind tricks? That was the best explanation I had, but even I didn't believe it. That memory with him . . . it felt real. I felt it in my heart. My soul.

Pan cupped my cheek. "Adora, say something. I need you to focus."

"I'm okay," I said, my voice cracking slightly on the way out. I cleared my throat and nodded. "Yeah, I'm good. Just taken by surprise. Not thrilled about it." *Part truth.*

Relief shone in his eyes, but then he pressed his lips together, trying to remain stoic as he had been before. "I don't want to risk another encounter. We need to take a different path."

"You won't hear any argument from me." I shuddered, thinking about the misshapen shifters and the weird flashes I experienced. "There's been entirely too much death since I got here." *All truth.* I was just thankful this latest group hadn't included any children.

Pan lingered for a moment, and I held his gaze. Warmth bloomed in my chest, telling me I'd found something I'd been searching for. The moment his hand left my face, a longing for his touch pulled at me.

I reached up and dug my fists into my eyes, rubbing like

this was a headache I could make go away. What the hell was wrong with me? Becoming one of those insipid women that developed feelings for a moody alphahole they'd just met.

Gag.

I knew myself better than that.

Whatever was happening to me had to do with this place, and whatever mystery it held. Part of me wanted to figure it out. Part of me wanted to take a nap and pretend this wasn't happening.

I had to settle for a long walk deep in my thoughts.

Not exactly a good place to be.

CHAPTER 7

PAN

I REPLAYED THE EARLIER ENCOUNTER ON A DESPERATE LOOP. AN inkling of hope fluttered, but I didn't dare acknowledge its presence. If I did, it would infect me with its poison. I'd fall for her again. I always did.

For a brief moment, I was sure she felt the spark between us. Or maybe it was just the bloodlust, a semblance of her true self returning the more she killed . . . but I was starting to believe that less and less.

There was a voice in my head that kept insisting she was different this time. The woman fighting in the jungle wasn't the same woman I'd known. The things she'd said didn't make sense. Guilt didn't mean you deserved to die? That wasn't Kali's viewpoint. It wasn't in her nature to be forgiving. She was brutal. Ruthless.

She hadn't spoken since we'd left and taken an alternate path, determined to keep quiet. Her screams had given away our location when she'd fallen down the embankment. Clearly she wasn't going to let anything like that happen again and risk alerting further shifters. She spoke not a word. Not a complaint. Not a question. Just silence.

"We'll be at the ruins shortly," I said, glancing at her.

"The where?"

"The ruins. It's a shorter path to the caves," I answered.

She slowed her pace, turning to me. "Don't people usually live near ruins? Places like that provide shelter. Civilizations are built near natural resources, so won't more shifters be living in that area?"

I inhaled deeply, letting it out slowly. "Not these ruins. No one goes there. They believe they're haunted."

She let out an annoyed scoff. "I can deal with haunted, but if it's a shortcut and no one is there, why didn't we take that way before?"

Because I didn't want to. Because it is a painful reminder of the past. I couldn't explain that to her. Maybe I wouldn't have to. Being back there might trigger her memories even more. I'd be lying to myself if I said I wasn't terrified of seeing her that way again.

After a while, the jungle started to thin out, and a clearing appeared not far from our path. As we broke through the tree line to open ground, the view changed. A large, flat area spread in front of us. The once-vibrant green grass was still dead and blackened, never able to grow again after the destruction of this place. The foliage surrounding it wasn't as thick as one would expect, and younger trees grew at its edge, trying to reach the height of their neighbors. But the centerpiece was the ruins positioned on a plateau, steep cliffs on either side. The moonlight cast the entire scene in an eerie glow.

"Holy shit," she breathed, her eyes wide as she took it in. "It looks like a bomb went off here," Adora muttered, kneeling down and rubbing the charred ground with her hand. She lifted her fingers to her nose and sniffed. She looked at me in confusion. "There's no smell."

I tilted my head, considering her. "What were you expecting?"

She pressed her hands to her thighs and pushed herself to stand, then she shrugged. "An accelerant of some sort, or the scent of magic."

I stared at her blankly for a few moments, trying to register what she'd said. "You can *scent* magic?"

She crossed her arms and cocked an eyebrow. "You seem to be shocked again, Mr. God-king. You act like a know-it-all, but you don't really know much about me."

I gave her a deadpan look, and she rolled her eyes in return.

"Yes, I can scent magic."

"Peacocks can't do that." *She* couldn't do that.

"Well, I don't know what other peacocks can supposedly do. I'm the only one left on Earth, so I've been on my own there, and *I* can scent magic. My moms taught me how. I'm not that great at it, mind you, but I can get by okay. It comes in handy working with the Portal Guard. Investigating and whatnot. An explosion like this should be easy. It's hard to mask the scent for something of this magnitude, but there was nothing."

It had been an immense explosion. Those who didn't feel the tremors in its wake were rocked to their core by the devastation and loss. All of Arcadia felt it in some manner. I felt it still.

"We're losing the cover of night," I said, glancing at the dim streak of sun on the horizon. "The caves are at the base of the valley below, just on the other side of these ruins and down a very long set of stairs that I'm not looking forward to descending. So let's go."

Adora pressed her lips together as she stared at the remnants of the structure, massive even in decay. Columns that once stood high were now toppled and broken. Huge rectangular stones littered the ground, and some had clearly fallen over the edge of the cliffs. "Stairs? In that? It doesn't look structurally sound. Is there a way to climb down the side?"

"The only way is through it, unless you want to fly." She was already full of surprises and liked to point out how little I knew about her. Perhaps this was one of those times.

She frowned. "Peacocks aren't exactly graceful in flight," she started, trailing off as she peered over the edge. The ravine was steep, and sharp rocks jutted from the mountainside. "I'll pass. Last time I tried to fly, I couldn't do it without hitting a tree. And that was ten feet off the ground."

"Wise choice." I took the steps that led up into the ruins and pulled down a torch mounted on the wall. Snapping my fingers, a small fire lit on its top, casting a warm glow around us.

She raised her eyebrows in disbelief, then gave me a look of approval. "Fancy."

I took a deep breath before entering. I wasn't ready, but this was the only way to avoid killing any more of my people. Adora followed silently, and I turned my head to see her in my periphery. She looked around, cautious and curious, her hand on her dagger.

"You won't need that here." When she gave me a questioning look, I jutted my chin to the hand on her weapon.

"You say that," she whispered, her eyes still shifting from side to side as though she were waiting for someone to jump out. "And yet . . ."

Step by step, we made our way through the expansive entrance. Our footfalls made soft thuds as we walked through the eerie darkness, but it wasn't long before the sounds within these haunted walls changed. A sick crunching rose as the weight of our bodies crushed the bones beneath us. My stomach tightened with grief, and I wanted more than anything to be away from it.

"Pan?" Her voice remained steady, but there was a nervousness in her tenor. "What are these ruins of?"

"A temple."

"What happened here?" The words were barely audible, and she'd stopped walking. I turned to see her looking at the ground, waiting for me to answer. She looked up, her brows pinched together, fear written all over her face.

"Death. That's what happened."

"Stop being a cryptic asshole and answer me," she demanded, her voice wavering as it rose in pitch with her anger. "What. Happened?"

I sighed. "The goddess of destruction happened." Stepping toward her brought the light of the torch closer. As I approached, the flames flickered, casting our shadows on the wall . . . and illuminating the bones and skulls that littered the temple floor.

Her mouth fell open as she took in the sheer number of dead that called this their final resting place. Adora kneeled down, picking up a small skull and holding it in the palm of her hands. She looked over, seeing another and comparing their similar sizes. Crawling on the floor, she came to another. And another. And another. Every bone she picked up, every skull, she saw how small it was.

I stood there and watched, saying nothing.

She stared up at me, her eyes glittering with tears. "They're all children, Pan. *Thousands* of them. Why?" Her breath shuddered as she spoke.

I held the torch up, pointing to the faded murals on the walls. "At the base of this ruin, in the valley, there was once a civilization. A peaceful people, they thrived here for generations. They weren't warriors. They were farmers. Families. Scholars. Free thinkers." I turned my arm so the flames would light up another mural, showing families working together. "The goddess of destruction demanded they worship her, but they refused, protesting against a religion they didn't believe in. They argued for their right to teach free thought. So she destroyed them for it, setting an example first by filling the temple with children then collapsing it."

Adora gasped, clutching the small bone she held in her hand. She craned her head, looking all around at what was left of the dead. "Why? What kind of monster just . . . just kills children? For the sake of her fucking vanity . . ."

As the tears tracked down her face, I felt the sincerity radiate from her. The pain. The sadness. All the unfamiliar emotions were jarring to watch when I realized this was all genuine. There was no agenda. No trickery or false pretenses. Adora was genuinely heartbroken at what she saw. At what she'd just learned.

And that rocked me, to see her like this.

She sat there and wept, clutching a small finger bone to her chest as she grieved for those she didn't know.

I dropped to my knee, resting my arm on my thigh. Reaching out, I cupped her cheek, then wiped the tears from her face with my thumb as she looked up at me.

"I didn't know being here would hurt you," I ventured, trying to think of what to say. "If I'd have known . . ."

She quickly moved to her knees, throwing her arms around my neck and nearly knocking me over with the force of her embrace. She cried noiselessly on my shoulder for a moment while I remained in my crouched position. With my arm wrapped around her lower back, I held her to me.

Her ombre blue hair brushed my skin, and the scent of her triggered memories with her that I'd tried to shove away. What we were like when she *wasn't* the monster. When she had been a friend. When we'd been lovers.

What was happening now surpassed even that.

In every other lifetime, she'd never been empathetic. She'd never loved anyone beyond herself. I'd often questioned if she even truly loved me, though I never wanted to know the real answer.

Stroking her hair, I waited until she pulled away from me. She wiped her cheeks, smearing the dirt that covered them. Adora nodded while she pushed herself to stand. "Can we just go?"

I inclined my head. "The stairs aren't far from here."

"Is there anything I need to know before we get there? I can handle it; I just need to know what I'm walking into."

"It's a long staircase, and the way is dark. Stay close to me, but don't try to look over the railing," I said after a moment of thought.

"That's where the adults are, isn't it?" she asked. I pressed my lips together and confirmed her suspicion with a single nod. "Got it."

"We'll be there soon. Then you can rest."

She straightened her shoulders and gestured for me to lead the way. She'd put on a strong face, acting unbothered by the atrocities of these ruins. With her features schooled, you'd never know she'd cried or cared. The logical part of me argued that *this* was the reaction I'd expected, this was the real her. Callous. Heartless. Cruel.

I wanted to believe it.

And I could have convinced myself if I hadn't heard her quietly sniffling as we descended in silence, surrounded by the souls of the dead that still haunted the ruins.

CHAPTER 8
ADORA

I COULD SMELL THE WATER BEFORE WE ARRIVED. THAT DELIGHTFUL crisp and fresh scent reached my nose, and I inhaled, taking it all in and imagining what it would be like to feel clean again.

I was so over this day.

I'd started to question my instincts. Did peacocks have good instincts? I didn't know. I'd always trusted myself. Danni had trusted me. Now I wasn't so sure.

Nothing was right in Arcadia. Of course, we'd already known that on our side of the portal, but not to such an extent. I would have never guessed it was filled with mutant, half-shifted inhabitants that had become feral and attacked without provocation. I thought that was the worst of it, but walking into the temple ruins tore at my soul.

My entire life, I'd put on a strong face. Where Dannika wore her heart on her sleeve, I hid behind a mask of indifference. I showed people what I wanted them to see. It wasn't false. It just wasn't all of me. Dannika was kinder, and I was meaner; there was no doubt about it. I stabbed first and asked questions later, while she weighed her options—but we both felt *deeply*. Maybe it had something to do with us being born during the Great Sacrifice—a night when my entire race was slaughtered, and her father was murdered. Maybe a piece of that pain and suffering our loved ones endured had become ingrained within us somehow.

Still, even with all my practice, there was no way to disguise my emotions when I held those tiny bones in my hand. I sensed an inexplicable familiarity in the ruins. The air was thick with sorrow and loss, so much so it was hard to breathe. The truth was that it was almost unbearable. It was easy to see why Arcadians would say it was haunted and no one dared to enter. I had a better understanding of why Pan didn't want to go there either. If I felt it, he surely did as well.

A deeper part of me wanted to avenge them. I just didn't know why. I wouldn't pretend that I was benevolent, or that I didn't hold grudges. I kept a list of those who'd done my family wrong, and some of them deserved to end up on the pointy end of a blade given the chance, but not for something as stupid and trivial as them not liking me. Not *worshipping* me. I was disgusted by the goddess that had inflicted pain and destruction on so many innocents for such a slight.

As we descended the staircase at the back of the temple, I made a silent vow to the souls of those murdered children: if I found the one responsible, I'd do everything in my power to put an end to her. To make sure she could never harm anyone ever again.

Reaching into my pocket, I touched the tiny bone I'd picked up. A metacarpal, as best as I could tell. Maybe a finger, depending on the age of the child. It didn't matter, really. I'd kept it as a reminder.

I didn't know why it had affected me so viscerally. Maybe it was because I'd lived my life believing I was the last of my kind. On Earth, I was. All because of self-righteous zealots who wanted to rule over others. Peacocks were deemed too dangerous because of the ability we'd inherited. With nothing more than a look we could see into someone's soul. See their past, their mistakes, their secrets. People who were stronger with more means didn't like the risk that posed, so we'd been exterminated as if we were ants and not people. *She* was no different, except this time, there were no survivors, and that made me sad. It was such a basic word to describe my emotion, but there was no other way to put it.

"You're awfully quiet." Pan's voice broke me away from my thoughts. "What are you doing?"

Plotting murder, but I don't plan on telling you that.

"Thinking about a bath."

He smiled, pointing ahead. "Right through there."

I looked up, catching sight of the cave entrance.

"Thank the gods," I breathed. *Not that bitch of destruction, though. Fuck her. I'll thank her for nothing.*

Running ahead, I entered. Dark shadows and a damp scent filled the space. I dropped to my knees, scooping my hands into the spring and bringing them to my mouth to drink over and over again. I took my fill before I stood up, stripping my shirt over my head.

"What are you doing?" Pan asked, his voice almost panicked. I glanced at him to see he'd backed away slightly. His brows were scrunched as he looked at me with suspicion.

"That's not usually the reaction I get when I take my clothes off," I said, shimmying my shorts down my legs. "But I guess there's a first time for everything."

He opened his mouth to talk again, but I didn't stick around to listen. I bundled my clothes under my arm and padded over to another pool, one I didn't plan to drink from, and dipped my toes in. A lukewarm temperature greeted me, and I walked right in, dropping until I was completely submerged.

The water rushed over my head, and I held my breath in the blissful silence until my lungs started to burn.

When I broke the surface, I noticed Pan had started a small fire near the cave entrance. He turned to look at me, aware that I was watching him.

"Why are you afraid of me?" I asked, rubbing my clothes together to wash the grime off of them as best I could. It didn't bother me that he didn't want to screw me, but the way he acted made me curious.

My comment made him bristle, and he straightened his back. "I'm not afraid of you," he said stiffly.

I gave him a flat glare. "C'mon, I just took off my clothes, and you took three steps back from me like my vagina has teeth."

His lips parted slightly, but something like a smile crept up one side of his mouth. After a moment, he said, "If we're going to be honest, I thought you were trying to seduce me."

Treading water, my head tipped back as I barked a laugh. I couldn't help myself. "If I wanted to seduce someone, coating myself in sweat, mud, leaves, and blood wouldn't be my first choice. Nothing sexier than rank body odor and open wounds," I said, lifting my arm and pointing to the gouges the puma left on my deltoid. The movement pulled at the wet cuts, and I winced.

Pan's expression softened. "I suppose that's a fair point."

"You know, when I first met you and you grabbed me by the neck and pressed your dick into my back, I gave the green light. But you declined. I can take no for an answer." I tilted my head to the side, then gestured at my arm and back. "That being said, I would be grateful for some help washing these. I don't heal as fast as you do. No naked funny business, I promise." I smiled, winking at him.

It was his turn to laugh, and I was pleased he seemed to chill out some after my comment. A tingling sensation ran over my exposed skin as the sound echoed in the cave. His mirth filled me with an emotion I couldn't place. I tossed my partially clean clothes onto the rock ledge so I could twist them out and dry them by the fire. Moving a little closer toward the shoreline, my feet found purchase, and I was able to stand. The water came to my breasts, barely covering my nipples.

Turning around, I looked at a wall in the back of the cavern. "See? I won't even look. Take off your pants, or don't. I'll never know." I was a total liar. Not about the seducing part. No was no, but I was one hundred percent going to check out the goods.

Pan chuckled, and I heard his pants rustle. Turning my head slightly, I glanced out of the corner of my eye to see what he had to offer. My mouth fell open, and I whipped my head around as quickly as possible. *Oh my gods . . . was that real? Are all gods endowed that way? Or just him? Is it an animal thing? No, I've been with average-sized shifters. That monster looks like it wouldn't fit. Not that I wouldn't give it a ride just to feel it out.*

The water splashed as he entered—the pool, not me— and he waded through until he made it to my spot.

"I know you looked," he said casually as he approached with his thin white shirt in hand.

I shrugged, turning around. "I was curious."

Once I was facing him, my stomach tightened. His eyes met mine, and we stared at each other in a tense silence. I meant what I'd said. He wasn't interested, and I was good with it, but my insides screamed at how much I *wanted* him. Trying to shake off the feeling, because I would never be *that* girl, I did the best thing I could think of. Talk about something gross.

"I, um—" My voice was breathy, which was not what I intended. I cleared my throat. "I don't want these cuts to get infected. Slower healing means they'll fill with pus and smell bad, so . . ."

Pan pressed his lips together in an attempt to not laugh at me, then managed to school his features. Guess maybe he saw through my subtle attempt to ignore my baser instincts. *So smooth, Adora.*

"What happened here?" Pan asked, pointing to just below my collarbone. His fingers traced a jagged, puffy scar, then touched the round scar next to it.

Flashbacks strobed in my thoughts, and emotions flared within. "I was captured by some assholes and stabbed. Probably wouldn't have scarred so badly had one of them not dug his grubby finger into it. Then they shot me."

Anger flashed in Pan's eyes. He tried to cover it, but I could see it clear as day.

"Who did this?"

"It doesn't matter anymore. They tried to kill my sister. They failed. We won." I shrugged, thinking back to that night.

Pan pressed his lips together, accepting my answer and not pushing further. "I don't think these will scar, but your healing should be better than this . . ."

"Really?" Curiosity filled me. "Do peacocks heal better when they're in Arcadia? Is this just because I'm so used to being on Earth? Like it drained my powers?"

"Sort of," he said softly, gently guiding my shoulder to turn me around. Water splashed against my skin, and he gently rubbed his wet shirt over my back. "It'll come back to you soon . . ." His voice trailed off in a somber tone.

For several minutes, he washed me slowly, taking care around the marks that hadn't quite healed.

"Tell me about life in your realm," he said. "I want to know more about you."

"I told you some things about me, remember? Then you wouldn't return the favor."

He dipped the fabric in the water before wringing it out and using it again. "You didn't tell me what you were doing on the other side of the portal."

"If I talk about me, will you answer my questions?" I turned my head slightly to look at him from my periphery.

He smirked, keeping his eyes focused on his work. "Some of them, yes."

It was better than none. "I joined the Portal Watch. We're the faction that guard the portals between realms. There's seven of them on Earth. There's this one to Arcadia, of course, Celestia that goes to a world of angels and demons, Faery goes to the fae—obviously, unpronounceable portal is in the Himalayas—"

"Unpronounceable portal?" He repeated, amusement lining his tone.

"It's the language of the gods—or at least the god-like entities that come out of it. That portal sucks. It's freezing. The Watch there are mostly arrogant fucks that think they're better than the rest of us because they guard the most inhospitable portal with the most powerful beings." I rolled my eyes. "The world on the other side blows anyway. Not that they know that. We're technically not supposed to cross that one . . ."

"But you've never been one for following the rules?" Pan guessed.

"In my defense, some jackass dared me to because he thought I'd chicken out. I made him my bitch the remaining three weeks I was there." Pan chuckled quietly, his warm breath doing things to my skin I wasn't supposed to think about. "Anyway, then there's the witch portal in the Sahara, Vuulectus in the land down under, and Oceania in the Pacific. Oceania is the only one I haven't been to. Kinda hard to get an invite when it's a few hundred feet underwater. That one is mostly left to Sea and Serpentine to do what they want since they're the only House that can easily access it. The other six we monitor the comings and goings of supernaturals. Protect our world when something undesirable comes through. That sort of thing. When I finished my training, I chose to return to Portland to guard the Arcadian portal."

"Are you happy there?" he asked, gently lifting my injured arm from the water and skimming the cloth over it with care.

"I don't know. Sometimes? No one there even knows what kind of shifter I am, except for my family. The peacocks were slaughtered because the Eyes of God. I was told that they refused to be controlled. Their power was heavily coveted, but they wouldn't yield. Since they couldn't be used as a weapon, they were killed. My family kept my secret, but I can't trust that anyone else will when push comes to shove. So I don't get close to anyone. Most of the time I'm good with it, I suppose, but it can get lonely."

My honest admission shocked me. I hadn't ever said that out loud before.

He hummed in response, placing the palm of his hand onto my deltoid. Warmth pressed into my skin, sending tingles over my body. "I know how that feels, actually. More than you can imagine."

When he lifted his hand, the gashes were now faint scars. I touched it, looking up at him. "How'd you do that?"

"It's a power bestowed to only those that are called 'Entitled Ones.'"

I twisted my lips. "Fair enough. It's my turn to ask questions." I held my hand out, but he just stared at me confused. "The cloth, please. I know your wounds are healed, but the least I can do is help you clean up. You're covered in blood too." My eyes drifted to his tanned skin, looking down at his arms and seeing the remnants of our earlier battles.

He dipped his chin, turning around.

"Tell me about your world before this madness took over. Before your bitch of destruction started leveling temples," I suggested, choosing to make a statement rather than ask a question. I thought it might help him open up.

His muscles tensed, but I remained quiet, gently cleaning the dirt and blood from his back.

Finally, he sighed. "It was a happier place. There's not much more to it, really. When she is here, the world falls into darkness after a time. There's nothing I can do about it, I've learned, and my people suffer for it. No matter what I do, it seems."

"Where is she now?"

"Gone." It was his only answer, and the sadness in that singular word danced across my skin.

"Gone?" I pressed. "Like, she's visiting her family in Fiji, or she's dead? Do goddesses even die?" *Please tell me this one did.*

He chuckled slightly, but it was halfhearted, the movement creating tiny ripples in the spring. "This one can die, yes, but she always comes back."

I traced the cloth down the length of his arm, taking care to make sure the skin was free of impurities. My hand followed in its wake, rinsing off as I went. "How can she come back from the dead? That seems awfully convenient. Is she a necromancer?"

"No, she has a temple that keeps her reincarnating. While I am the god-king of this world, she was created to be my equal counterpart. To balance me should I ever . . . lose control. Except it ended up being the opposite. Somewhere along the way, the fates that created us both made a mistake. While I cannot die, she can, but whenever an act of injustice occurs that triggers her magic, she's reborn. Her temple has made it so that she's stronger with each lifecycle."

"A temple? That's it?" I repeated, raising my voice a bit. "Well, if she's always destroying people, why don't you return the favor? Destroy her temple and kill her for good?"

Pan turned as I finished washing his back, and when I moved to wash his chest, he held my hand in place, keeping his eyes focused on me. "I can't destroy it. No one can," he whispered. "It's tied to her in a way that magic can't break. She's the only one who can destroy it, and she never will."

I could see how much pain he was in, and it tore me apart inside. Reaching up, I placed my hand on his cheek, staring into his swirling green eyes. I couldn't help the strong desire to use my power. I wanted to see into him. I wanted to know more, but as I released a piece of my magic, his eyelids narrowed a fraction.

"I can feel you trying," he said, cupping my hand. "I won't let you in."

I frowned. "You're keeping something from me. I just want to understand. I want to help."

"And what would you do to help, if you could?"

"I don't know, maybe light her on fire?" I suggested. "We have really good pyrotechnics on Earth. I know a warlock, he's a fuc—err, a friend who experiments with magically enhanced dynamite. I'm just saying, it's worth a shot."

"Why do you care so much?" He asked, searching my gaze. "I've been an ass to you most of this trip. The people here have done nothing but try to kill you. Why do you care what happens to us, them, if the goddess of destruction returned?"

"I don't like bullies. My sister Danni was bullied horribly when we were kids, all because she couldn't shift. I took the punches that I could, but if I got in the way they just hurt her twice as bad when I wasn't there. I felt helpless. So, I can relate to the way this hurts you. I want you to be free of that, even if you are an ass. I can't fix this curse myself, but you'll get your animal souls back when you return me. I'm sorry my . . . kind have been such dicks, but I want your people to be free of their cursed bodies and able to shift as one. I want this world to recover. If what you say is true and this goddess of destruction will come back, they're going to need you at your best even more."

"You almost give me hope," he said so quietly I nearly missed his words.

"Almost?" I asked, trying to cool the flames that were slowly eating at me.

"I've been around too long to wonder how it ends."

I nodded slowly. "Maybe you're too old and set in your

ways, but I'm not. This time you have the portal to Earth. Maybe those same fates that screwed you decided to throw you a bone?" My lips curled up in a half smile as he stared at me with something I didn't want to name.

"You continue to fascinate me, Adora," he whispered, caressing my hand. "You are so much more than I expected."

As I stood in front of him, I could no longer ignore the fact that something drew me to him. Sliding my hand around to the back of his head, I guided him toward me, pulling his face to mine. I paused when only a hairsbreadth stood between us. Drunk on the scent of him, I still let the moment settle in, giving him every opportunity to turn me away. To stop this.

Pan's eyes flashed, showing something I thought I'd only ever imagined when he looked at me. Hunger.

He inhaled abruptly when our lips met, and a jolt of energy passed between us. I pressed against him, feeling a familiar ache between my legs, wanting so badly to take whatever this was a step further. My animal called to him, begging to be filled. She wanted his lingering gaze and unrestrained passion. His rough hands and gentle caresses.

My fingers threaded through his hair as I opened my mouth to him, my other hand resting against the planes of his chest. His cock swelled in the water, pressing into my belly.

He kissed me hungrily, sucking my bottom lip and scraping it with his teeth as he pulled away before covering my mouth with his once more.

I craved him, and I knew if I didn't pull away, I wouldn't stop. He'd said no—and I wouldn't cloud his judgment.

I broke the kiss, sliding my arms between us to create space. The moment I did, my body screamed and yearned to be close to his again. Shaking my head and wiping off my lips with a wet hand, I knew I needed to explain myself. "You, um, you didn't want this to happen, and I said it wouldn't. I don't know what came over me." I couldn't find it in myself to say I was sorry. I wasn't sure it was true. Not if I wanted so badly to turn around and start it all over again. So I went with truth. "I didn't mean to be a cock tease. Honest. That's not my style, and I'm sorry for that. Truly."

I ran my fingers through my hair, unable to read the expression on his face. Guilt? Anger? Desire? I had no idea. I took some steps around him as I walked to the shoreline.

Halfway there, a hard body pressed against my back, molding to fit me. My breath stuttered in my chest as his cock pressed into the cleft of my ass. Rough fingers grasped my hip bone, squeezing hard enough to leave marks. His other hand wound itself around my hair. Air hissed between my teeth as he pulled it to one side sharply, forcing my head with it.

Heat burned in my core.

"Pan . . ."

Lips slid up the column of my throat to the hollow of my ear. My breathing turned erratic as the flat edge of his teeth nipped my earlobe.

Pleasure shot from his bite straight down my body. I pressed my thighs together. The slickness running down them had nothing to do with the water.

"I'm not known for my self-control," I breathed. "If you turn me on then leave me hanging, I *will* finish the job myself, even if you're in this cave when I do it."

"I . . ." His gruff voice trailed as my back arched, pressing my ass into him. "I won't fuck you."

Ice water doused my veins, followed by a different kind of fire.

I pulled away from him—or tried to. The hand in my hair tightened, yanking me back to his chest.

"What the hell is wrong with you?" I snapped.

"So much," he breathed against my neck. He cursed in that language that I should not know but somehow did. "I can't fuck you. Not when . . ."

I craned my neck as far as I could to look at the man who held me in his arms. "Spit it out or let me go. You turned me down, and I said I don't know what came over me. You had the go-ahead, but you don't want it. Fine. But acting like this when I *want* you and you know it. That's just cruel."

Pan sighed. "I can't," I started to shake my head in disbelief, and he pulled my hair taut again. Forcing me back against his chest. "But if I let you go right now without feeling your sweet cunt come on my fingers, I know I'll regret it and I already live with too many regrets."

I stilled in my fight, far too agreeable for how cagey that answer was. "So what? I'm good enough to finger bang but not actually fuck? This after you acted like I had some sort of disease when I gave you the greenlight?"

"That's not it."

"Bullshit."

He growled, the sound rumbling through his chest where it pressed into my skin. "It's not a question of want, Adora." His cock thrust against my ass. Hard. Heavy. "I can't fuck you because I would impregnate you whether I wanted to or not. I'm the god of Arcadia itself. The land lives because I live. You're a shifter in my domain, where I'm most fertile. The pullout method won't work. Neither would human contraceptives."

Understanding grounded me to the spot.

"Oh."

"Now do you see?"

"Yep, and thanks for not doing that. This is a no-god-spawn-factory."

His nose ran up my neck as he laughed lightly. "No-god-spawn-factory?"

"No mini-entitled ones."

"Hate to break it to you, but all children are entitled. Not just godly ones. Comes with being reliant on—"

"You know what I mean, asshole. Now are you going to help me or are you going to ruin the moment and I'll go take care of myself?"

Pan didn't waste any more time. Spinning me so fast I was dizzy, he grabbed my thighs where they met my ass and lifted me against him. Our naked bodies pressed together. Chest to chest.

His thick cock touched my spread pussy with every step but never near my entrance. With other guys, I might have worried about the precarious position, given the number of asshats that preferred to go bareback regardless of the consequences. Pan wasn't like that.

He took care to never push the line while still teasing me. Sparks of ecstasy zipped along my skin everywhere he touched.

My back touched a hard rock surface.

"Lift your hands," he commanded. I arched an eyebrow but did as he said. Almost instantly something tough and leathery wrapped around my wrists. I frowned, arching my back to tilt my head up and see. Ancient vines in hues of blue and brown wrapped around my wrists and arms.

Pan kissed my neck, nibbling at my skin. His hands ran

up and down my thighs as the vines took a hefty portion of my weight, pulling my shoulders taut.

He pushed my legs wider, spreading me further than I'd ever been. My muscles tingled with the edge of a burn just as something collared each ankle. I gasped as vines pushed out from the cave wall to wrap around each calf and thigh. My upper half was suspended while the lower was locked in place and unable to move an inch.

Pan took a couple of steps back. His green eyes flashed with raw hunger. He closed his hand in a fist and bit down on the edge of it as he took me in.

"You planning to stand there and stare like a creeper, or—"

An earthy musk washed over my senses as a vine wrapped around my face, tightening at my mouth like a gag.

Holy shit.

I was pretty sure a waterfall of my own making gushed from between my thighs. My cheeks heated as I felt my own slick arousal running down my inner thighs.

Pan grinned with pure male satisfaction. "Snap your fingers if it becomes too much," he directed.

I nodded; or tried to.

Pan approached. One rough hand cupped my breast, fingers tweaking the nipple. I jerked. Need shot straight from my breast to my core, reminding me of its emptiness —and how much I desired for him to fill me.

"That tiny little tank top you call a shirt has been taunting me for days," he said, lowering himself to my breast. He took my nipple between his lips and sucked the already tight peak until it was so sensitive, even his breath made it tender.

His thumb gently brushed over it and I cried out against my makeshift gag.

"Such a needy little thing . . ." He repeated the process to the other side, smirking when I began to writhe against my restraints.

Fingertips trailed down my belly, curving around the crease where my thigh met my hip. Those tortuous fingers skimmed the edge of my folds, and a groaned rumble ran through him. "Fuck. You're *dripping*."

Pan dropped to his knees. His nose skimmed from the corner of my knee, up my inner thigh. He stopped just short of where I wanted him and bit down. Not hard enough to break skin, but it would definitely bruise.

Desire pulsed in the air; so thick and all-consuming, I felt like I'd die from it.

It's like he knew every place to touch that would drive me insane.

Then I felt his tongue lick inside me.

Heat rushed to my head, as I reached for the release that was too far out of my control. "I'll never get this taste out of my head," he groaned, then penetrated deep again.

I thrashed against the vines that held me tight, but it didn't hurry him along. Pan took great pleasure in licking and sucking everywhere . . . except the spot where I needed him most. I twisted my wrists and flexed my strength, but it did no good. Whatever plant these vines were made of were stronger than what we had on Earth. That or his magic made them unbreakable.

Pan shifted his tongue to my swollen clit. He hadn't touched it, but gods did I need him to. He traced light circles around it with the very tip of his tongue, making my indignation evaporate. If he'd asked me to beg right then, I would have.

My teeth sank into the smooth wood-like plant that gagged me. The slight taste of mint with coconut touched my tongue, along with something unknown.

Pan stilled. "Keep those teeth sheathed or I'll give you something to chew on."

He could feel that?

Damn. He really was one with the planet.

Little did he know, I'd like that.

As if reading my thoughts, Pan looked up, his eyes filled with lust. "Darling, when I'm done here, you won't be able to keep your head up—let alone suck my cock."

Then he sucked my clit into his mouth and shoved two blunt fingers in me at the same time.

I came apart. Black touched the corners of my vision, eating it up. My world narrowed to one singular thing.

Pan.

His tongue did something to me that made my entire body seize. Darkness took me as I orgasmed harder than I ever had before.

I was so fucked.

CHAPTER 9

PAN

I spent most of the day watching her sleep, thinking about what had happened between us.

I'd been wrong about her. Again. Something in me snapped the moment I realized her motives were organic. The kiss was just that. A kiss. And gods, her lips felt good. She tasted different this time. Hungry. Experienced. Raw. New. A multitude of words came to mind as her taste lingered on my tongue.

Who was this fascinating and beautiful creature?

I couldn't stop myself after that. I ate her pussy half a dozen times, to the point that she was crying from over-stimulation before I finally let her down and put her to sleep. I retreated back to the pools to take care of myself after that, but it wasn't enough. I was hard the second I stepped back into her vicinity.

So like the inexperienced and overzealous young shifter she made me feel like— instead of the immortal being I was —I did it again and again until nothing more came out of me. I imagined my cock was between her parted lips instead of my fist, and I finally found some semblance of sanity.

I wasn't sated. Not even close, but it would have to do.

I wanted more of her. More time to know this version of her. But I knew what was at stake.

Arcadia in its entirety.

Still. It didn't make my heart's desires any less.

For over a hundred years I'd convinced myself I'd never trust her again. Never love her again. Now? I feared losing her, not to death, but to herself. All the emotions of the past came flooding back, but this time, it broke through my armor in a way I couldn't understand.

"You're watching me again," she whispered before cracking an eye open. "Creep."

I suppressed a laugh and instead smiled. "Maybe I am."

She'd slept naked, which did little for my raging hard on. I'd watched the rise and fall of her chest, the pebbling of her nipples as she turned and the cool stone sent goose-bumps over her warm skin, and the flutter of her eyelids as she dreamed.

I wanted little more than to be sheathed in her tight heat and see if she felt the same as before, or if that was new too. I couldn't bring myself to; not when she wasn't aware of who she was. What *we* had been.

I'd fed her half-truths that I knew would lessen the sting of me not fucking her.

She rolled over, her ombre blue hair spilling over her breasts before she sat up. As she glanced outside the cave, she saw the haze of the moonlight illuminating the entrance. "I overslept. Why didn't you wake me?"

"You needed more rest," I answered, pointing to her body. "Your wounds are all healed now."

She inspected her body, noticing how every scratch and

cut was gone, with fresh pink skin where the deepest gouges had been. She hummed in surprise. "Guess my blood *is* from this realm if my body is reacting this way. I never heal this fast at home."

I wondered if she'd remember her "home" for much longer. I shoved the thought away, offered her breakfast, and started the final leg of our journey.

"You said you're taking me to Atlantis, right?" she asked after we'd walked in silence for a time. She kept her voice low in fear of attracting more feral Arcadians, and I appreciated it more than she could imagine.

I nodded. "It won't be long."

"Are all peacocks from there?"

"No," I answered, shaking my head. "Peacocks came from all over Arcadia. They thrived. Their colors brightened this world. They were peaceful."

"You're talking about them in the past tense," she said slowly.

"The peacocks felt in danger here, and they all fled for safety. I couldn't protect them." An admission that haunted me, like so many other failures.

"The goddess?" she guessed, and I nodded in confirmation. "How many are left?"

"These three are the last that I know of, besides you."

"Are they all black like me?"

"No, you are the only black peacock to have ever lived." And the only one that ever would.

"Wow . . . really?" The realization filled her voice with awe and wonder. "And they live in Atlantis? Like, the Atlantis that sank into the sea? At least, that's how the story goes on Earth . . ." When she trailed off, she looked at me to fill in the gaps.

I worried I might tell her too much, but I knew she

couldn't piece it all together. She was missing crucial pieces of the puzzle that only I could give her.

"Atlantis didn't sink," I started, tilting my head to watch her reaction. "Not in the way you're likely thinking. It was razed by the goddess. It once held her worshippers, but like all evolving creatures, they had the ability to think. Analyze. Form opinions. When some dissented in their beliefs, she sent a tidal wave. I tried to stop her, like I always do. But I couldn't."

Adora snorted in derision. "That bitch really has an ego the size of Texas, doesn't she?"

"Texas?"

"An old territory on Earth. Big. Filled with mosquitoes and other things that want to kill you for no good reason." She waved her hand around as she spoke. "Kinda like here, the more I think about it."

I chuckled. Wonder consumed me. Would she be the same after she was taken by the priestesses? Would some of these qualities pass on to her? So much of her was different. I liked it. I wanted to keep her like this.

I wanted to keep her, period.

We walked in silence, but I found when she was quiet, I desired to know what was going on in her mind. Her thoughts were never what I expected.

"What are you thinking about?" I asked lightly.

"Meeting the other peacocks. I'm a little nervous and excited at the same time," she admitted.

Again. Never what I expected. "Nervous?"

She nodded, looking up at me with soulful brown eyes. "Wouldn't you be? I've never met any others like me. I have so many questions. But also, what if I don't fit in? What if they don't like my family?"

I almost stumbled. "Your family?"

"Well, yeah. I know the portal is wacky right now and I don't know much about how to fix that yet, but I figured maybe once you have Flora and Fauna back, the portal will be fixed, and I can bring them through to meet the peacocks." I slowed my pace, and it made her reduce her speed to match. "I . . . I wasn't planning on staying here permanently if there's a way back to them. I figured I'd live in both places. Maybe we could see each other more." Her fingers brushed against my arm lightly—her intention unmistakable. "You know, I mean, when you're not dragging me through the jungle on a blackmail-fueled quest."

Atlantis was just beyond the clearing. I didn't want to go further. If I did, this moment was over, and my insides clenched and coiled in turmoil.

When I didn't answer, she mistook my silence for rejection, and took hasty steps to put distance between us. "Or not, which is totally okay too—"

I grabbed her wrist, twirling her around and tugging her to me. She pulled her blade from her hip in an instant, reflexes kicking in over being grabbed.

Throwing out my other hand to catch her weapon-wielding arm, I held firm, pulling her in and crushing my lips to hers. Her tense body relaxed, melting into mine as I pushed my tongue into her mouth, savoring her taste, hoping I could burn it into my mind just like this.

Whatever this version of her was, I never wanted it to go away. I wanted her taste, her scent, her electrifying touch—I wanted it all to linger so I could call on the memory whenever I wanted.

Adora moaned, dropping the dagger and twining her arm around my neck as she stood on her tiptoes. My hands grazed up the curve of her hips, over the exposed skin of her waist, trailing her ribcage as we kissed like it was both our first and last kiss ever. Like we'd never see each other again. Never have the opportunity to feel this again.

A wave crashing against the rocks ahead startled us, and we broke apart. I looked into her heated gaze, following her tongue as it traced over her swollen lips. The sun started to crest over the horizon, painting a soft orange hue across the sky.

"I needed to do that," I managed, clearing my throat.

She nodded, breathless, closing her eyes while she grounded herself. "I'm not complaining."

"We're here." I took her hand, leading her to the water's edge. "Are you ready?"

I guided her over the stone steps that rose from the crystal clear water until they came to an end. She looked around, confused.

"What now?"

"Now, we swim. Follow me."

As we dove in, my heart tore itself into pieces.

My cynical self wanted to say I was back where I said I would never be again. My emotions raged against the very notion and said I'd never been with her before. Not like this.

The logical part of me knew what I had to do.

The logical part of me knew I had no choice.

The logical part of me still hated what was about to happen.

CHAPTER 10

ADORA

I COULD SEE LIGHT SHIMMERING THROUGH THE RIPPLES BENEATH the water. Fire. Torches.

Little bubbles escaped my nose, and my lungs began to burn. Kicking my legs harder, slicing my hands through the water to pull me closer to the exit ahead of us.

Peacocks. Family. They were *here*. Supposedly searching for me my entire life. So desperate to find me that they were willing to extort their god-king, charging him with the task. If that wasn't ruthless, I didn't know what was.

Honestly, it sounded like something I would do.

I would have blackmailed, begged, borrowed, stolen, or killed to find Danni if she'd been taken from me. I understood the sentiment, though I could see how others might find it cruel. The consequences for Arcadia certainly had been.

My heart squeezed at the idea of learning more about who I was. Where I had come from. Our culture. Traditions. Our history.

Would they be able to tell me about my peacock family on Earth? Did they know them? When had they crossed

103

from Arcadia into Portland? Did I have brothers or sisters still here? Cousins? I had so many questions. Anxiety and excitement warred within me.

But there was another emotion. One I didn't like.

A hesitation. A worry.

I heard it, and I knew better than to ignore it, but I still chose to. I couldn't live my life questioning where I came from.

And what had happened with Pan . . . I could try all I wanted, but the inexplicable pull and desire I felt toward him wasn't to be ignored. At least not on my part.

As I broke the surface, I sucked in a lungful of air, feeling my chest expand. I coughed slightly, sputtering water. Moments later, Pan appeared beside me, inhaling as soon as he was able. I glanced around the sunken room. The cavernous ruins were crumbling just as badly as the first temple had been. But where those ruins were an abandoned graveyard, this one looked inhabited. Lit torches lined the walls, and a set of steps led out of the water to a large rug. Another set of steps from there led to an unknown location.

"I win," I said between heavy breaths. I treaded water, staying afloat in the pool not three feet from him.

"What?" he asked, rubbing his eyes and trying to focus on me.

"I beat you. By a few seconds, sure, but I got here first." I smiled while he stared at me blankly.

"I didn't realize you were . . . racing," he said, shifting his gaze to the steps leading out of the water.

I splashed water at him. "You need to have more fun in life. Maybe I can teach you how."

His lips curled up in a hesitant smile.

It hit me that he was going to leave as soon as he

dropped me off. Whatever had just transpired between us —whatever that kiss was—it didn't share the same meaning to him. For me it meant possibility. For him, perhaps it was goodbye. If he was tasked with finding me against his will, I could understand not wanting to stick around, even with last night, but an emptiness settled in me at the knowledge that I probably wouldn't see him again.

I'd known him for all of three days, but I felt so deeply that he was a part of me somehow.

I didn't dare say that. I sounded like a lovesick lunatic.

Hey, we barely know each other, but I actually like you, and for some reason, you're stuck in my mind like you belong there and always have, so I'd really like it if you stayed with me.

I shook my head and almost laughed at myself.

No, those words wouldn't be coming out of my mouth.

I swam to the steps and got out of the water with Pan, standing beside him. I shuddered slightly, and he glanced at me.

"Are you okay?"

I nodded. "Just nervous."

"Do you feel anything . . . off?"

I instinctively looked down at my tattered, wet shirt. "I mean, if you're talking about my nipples sticking out through the shirt, yeah, I feel that. Not much can be done, I'm afraid. Unless you were talking about something else?" I angled my head to look at my backside and make sure I didn't have a gaping hole in the tiny cutoffs I wore. When I saw nothing, I faced him again. He looked lost for words, but a surprised grin washed over his face.

"You aren't what I expected." The melancholy in his tone was in stark contrast to the sparkle in his eyes, and it tugged at my heart. "For what it's worth, I've enjoyed our time together."

My brows furrowed. His goodbye was real. He really had no intention of seeing me again. I'd be lying if I'd said that didn't hurt. I'd had a teensy bit of hope that maybe he felt a connection to me too. All I could do was press my lips together in a forced smile and dip my chin.

As we took our first steps up the stairs, my heart began racing with anticipation.

Twelve steps left.

Nine.

Seven.

Three.

I stopped, reaching over to grab Pan's hand before we finished our climb. Before we met anyone and I lost the opportunity to say something to him in private.

As our skin made contact, electricity shot through me again. My entire body lit up like a Christmas tree. I felt it in my core. Between my legs. At my fingertips. I inhaled sharply, and my lips parted when I saw his pupils blown wide and his jaw clenched. He'd felt it too. It wasn't just me.

I stood there staring at him for a moment, not speaking, taking in my new realization.

"Pan," I started, trying to find the right words. "I wanted to say thank you for bringing me here. I'm sorry my family took Flora and Fauna from you. That you had to go through all this." When he started to speak, I cut him off so I could finish what I needed to say. "But I'm not sorry it was you that had to find me. I'm glad I got to be with you. I just . . . I just wish it could have been a little longer." I felt my voice quiver, and I cleared my throat. We'd kissed twice now. He brought me to release enough times that it quite literally knocked me out. We'd shared stolen touches and lingering gazes, but it wasn't enough. Something inside me yearned for more. Something inside me didn't want to leave his side. Acting on impulse, I pushed up on my toes and reached around his neck to pull him to me.

Our lips met in an impassioned kiss, and I inhaled sharply as he reciprocated instantly. His tongue traced my lips as I parted them, allowing him access to taste me further. His fingers laced through my hair, his other hand splaying across my lower back to keep me close. My body pressed against him, and I struggled for air. I'd been kissed before, but the intensity with which devoured me was going to make me see stars.

I moaned into his mouth, my tongue massaging his as I deepened the embrace. I pulled away too soon, grazing my teeth over his bottom lip, and kissing the corner of his mouth.

He pressed his forehead to mind, his eyes closed.

"Adora . . . we . . ." he started, trailing off. The way he was subtly pulling away from me stung, more than I ever wanted to admit after yesterday. I didn't understand it. One moment he was holding me to him, and the next he was putting up another barrier.

"It's okay, Pan. Really. In another life, right?" I said in jest with a humorless laugh, but the look on his face suggested I'd just slapped him. I held my arms out, smoothing my scraps of clothing. "How do I look?"

"Stunning."

I spun on my heel, taking the last few steps with Pan trailing behind me.

As I crested the top of the stairs, I saw a beautiful mosaic centered on the wall in front of me. Every vibrant and brilliant color I'd seen in the jungle for three days was represented. At its center was a temple raised up high, lording over all the meager people and villages depicted below it. Scripture was written to the sides in a language I didn't speak, but somehow still understood. Words that I shouldn't be able to read translated in my mind. *The Temple of Kali, goddess of destruction.* My fists tightened at my sides as my body shook. Above those damning words, brightly colored peacocks appeared to be in worship, circled around a single entity in the center . . . a black peacock.

My stomach roiled. Three days' worth of half-truths and lies sped through my mind. Pan's words echoed in my mind.

No, you are the only black peacock to have ever lived.

No . . .

"Pan?" I asked, but when I turned, he wouldn't look at me. I said his name again and again. He kept his gaze down, ignoring the fact that I was practically screaming at him.

"It is about time, Pan, god-king of shifters." A cold and monotone voice echoed in the cavern. I whirled around to see a woman in green robes, brown peahen feathers trailing behind her.

"Your demands are met. Give me back Flora and Fauna," Pan said, his words coming out tense and trembling.

"Demands? You did as you were commanded by the fates to do, Pan. We demanded nothing except what is *expected* of you," another scoffed. This one appeared exactly as the other did, identical in looks, but wearing gold robes.

"What are you talking about?" I whispered, turning to look at a third woman that had emerged from the shadows, her robes in shades of blue.

"It's—" Pan began, but the newest zealot spoke.

"It's his duty to bring you back to us. Those that held

you in that world kept you from your becoming. For years now, this land has suffered for it. Suffered for his sins."

I looked at Pan pleadingly. "Tell me it's not true."

When he couldn't speak, another answered. "Every lifetime you're reborn, Pan is charged with finding you and delivering you to us, your priestesses. This is the first he has delayed."

The words echoed in my head, drowning out other sounds as the chatter between them became fuzzy.

Every lifetime?

Finding me. Delivering me.

The whole time, I'd spilled my guts about my insecurities and desire for family. My longing for a place in the world. To know where I came from. Every tender touch and moment he gazed at me. The way he kissed me like his life depended on it . . . He'd led me on, bringing me here like a sacrificial lamb.

White-hot heat crept up my body, licking at my skin, kindling a flame inside me I'd never felt before. Rage unlike anything I'd ever known, fueled by unimaginable hurt.

"You tricked me," I hissed through clenched teeth. Taking a step toward him, he didn't move. He raised his chin in defiance.

"I didn't."

"It was all a lie." The room shook with the timbre of my voice. I'd never moved mountains with my anger before, but there was a first time for everything.

"Not all of it." He kept his gaze on me steady before his green eyes darkened, glancing at the priestesses behind me. "They are peacocks. They are your family. And they did want you back."

"Fuck your semantics."

"I'm sorry, Adora," he said quietly. "You have no idea how sorry I am."

"I don't believe you. You had three days to tell me the truth, Pan. Three! And you didn't. You can tell yourself whatever you want to feel better about it, but you carefully hid the truth from me. That's called lying."

"It is time, Kali," the green priestess said.

"Give me back Flora and Fauna," Pan shouted, his voice growing in strength and power. "I have returned her to you."

The three priestesses dipped their heads, chanting and moving their hands, looking like they were creating a spell. That was the closest thing I could relate it to. A burst of water sounded, and we all turned to the pool below. Two cages emerged from its depths, floating above the surface, and dissipating once they were over the stone dais.

Two wolves lay prone, and Pan rushed to their sides. Their bodies were lackluster, drenched, and unmoving. Until he touched them. In an instant, the wolves took on an effervescent quality. Pan's skin shimmered in a way it hadn't before. The misery and exhaustion on his face melted away. They stood, nuzzling his neck. They were whole again, the three of them, and Pan's power looked as though it had stabilized and returned.

He'd given me up for them. I wanted to hate him for it, but I knew how my sister and her wolf were bound to each other's souls. He did what he had to do, and I understood that through the deepest part of my anger. My shoulders sagged, and I took a painful breath.

"The Arcadians," I said softly, waiting for him to acknowledge me. When he did, I continued. "Will they become normal again? Proper shifters? Your magic . . . your power . . . If I stay here, will the madness that everyone has fallen into stop?"

He hesitated, his gaze shifting to the mosaic behind me, then he nodded slowly, and I understood what I had to do. My desire to leave this place, to fight my way out—I had to let it go. An entire realm suffered, and if I could save them from the nightmare they'd been living, I had to try. But this wasn't what I'd expected to find in my search. I never realized this would be my purpose. Noble as it might be to sacrifice oneself, it still sucked.

"Pan," I called out, and some of the sadness he'd worn returned when our eyes met. "Find my family. Tell them I love them and that I'm with other peacocks again. Tell them I'm okay so they never come looking for me. Do you understand? Lie to them like you lied to me. Don't let them cross into Arcadia. They can *never* know the truth."

"Adora, I—"

"Say you understand. Promise me this one thing. You owe me that much." I needed him to protect Danni, Nova, and my moms. They'd search for me, and I didn't know what they'd find. My heart ached when I thought of them, but it would shatter into a million pieces if I thought they'd get hurt looking for me. I'd almost lost Danni once, and it nearly destroyed me as I watched the life drain from her eyes. I needed to know she'd be okay. "Say it, Pan," I yelled, blinking furiously through my tears.

He set his jaw, his lips pressing into a thin, hard line. His nodded once, closing his eyes as he did. "I understand."

He turned, disappearing into the water with Flora and Fauna, and I stood unmoving until the water's surface settled again, not a ripple in sight.

A priestess laid her hand on my shoulder, and I flinched, disgusted by the contact. When her skin touched mine, it didn't elicit the electric buzz I felt with Pan. It wasn't tender like my mothers', or gentle and reassuring like my sister's. The touch was cold and sinister, causing me to pull away and sneer at her.

The priestess in gold walked to the mosaic, pressing a stone deep into the wall like a button. A loud groan sounded before a split appeared down the middle, parting into two door panels that swung inward.

Torches came to life on the wall, illuminating the hidden room.

Dark and rotted tree roots had broken through the ceiling. Black vines crept up through the cracks in the floor, wrapping themselves around the pillars that surrounded a large basin. Between each pillar, a curtain of water fell. A stale odor hit me, and I recoiled, coughing to the side.

"You've really kept up the place. Honest, it's the warmest welcome I could have imagined when I dreamed about what my long-lost family would be like." I walked forward, knowing full well they were going to tell me to go in anyway. "Nothing like eau de mildew and decay and . . . a tub filled with blood." I stopped dead in my tracks.

Horror filled me as I realized what the source of the rotting stench was. The contents of my stomach threatened to make an appearance, and I turned to the side, dry heaving as I doubled over, clenching my midsection.

"The fuck is wrong with you?" I choked out.

"It is time for your rebirth, Kali," the green-clad priestess said.

"My re-*what*?" I repeated, taking a step back, wiping my face with my forearm.

"Soon you will remember." The three peacocks pointed to the basin, signaling they expected me to get in.

"Um, there's no way in all the worlds and realms that I

am getting into that." I continued taking steps back. I knew I'd just had a moment of realization that I could save the tortured people of Arcadia, but that was before three psychos wanted me to get into a bath of blood. I had no intention of staying. There had to be another way to save them. Not to mention I'd rather drown in water trying to swim away than drown in *fucking blood.*

The priestess in blue robes chuckled, and the sound made my veins ice over. I couldn't move, and to my horror, I understood it wasn't a reaction. It was her using her magic on me. She was holding me in place while chanting, and the two other priestesses approached me and stood on either side and again, nausea washed over me.

My mind went to the finger bone in my pocket. I wouldn't become that. I couldn't. What that goddess had done . . .

Before I could process what that meant, the spell that held me lifted my body into the air, dragging me toward the sacrificial basin.

"Let me go!" My screams echoed off the walls, shaking the room as bits of sand and dust fell from the cracks. The gold priestess pulled a dagger from her robes and approached me as I hung in the air above the red expanse. I eyed the weapon, and then her. Hatred tore through me. "I will kill each and every one of you the first chance I get," I said, seething.

The peacock priestesses laughed in unison.

"You will forgive us when you return, Kali. You always do."

CHAPTER II
PAN

I sat on the edge of one of the floating stone steps leading to her temple. Flora and Fauna rested next to me, quiet and calm. They could feel my every emotion, though I imagined anyone could at this point. They didn't have to be the other half of my soul. The turmoil inside me was so intense, I was sure it radiated off me in waves.

"She is different this time," Flora spoke to me in my mind.

"That she is," I agreed, never taking my eyes off the mountain of stone that was her temple. I'd left her there, and I saw the hurt in her eyes when I did. She didn't understand why. Couldn't. I had seen her transformation countless times. I didn't want to witness it again.

"And yet you walked away from her, leaving her there with those power-hungry priestesses," Fauna stated. "It's clear you didn't want to."

"I had to," I whispered. "The realm has descended into madness without us. You were both aging. It might take a thousand years, but your deaths would be my end. Without us, Arcadia would fall. I had to make a choice."

Flora nudged my arm, scooting closer. "Then why do you sit here questioning your decision?"

I shook my head, not knowing how to put into words the struggle I felt within.

Fauna huffed, rolling her eyes, and breathing out harshly through her snout. "Because he loves her."

"I always love some part of her," I admitted. "We were made for a purpose."

"Oh, please," Fauna countered, tossing her head to the side. "She is different, so this love is different. We *feel* you, Pan. We are soul-bound. Stop lying to yourself. When you do, you lie to us in turn. It's beneath you."

"Fauna," her sister chastised. One kind and gentle, one straightforward and harsh. My yin and yang. "He's hurting."

I chuckled, relishing their company after how much I missed their bickering and comfort. "You're both right." Fauna licked her paw with pride.

"In truth, everything is different, isn't it?" Flora prodded. "I see her in your memories. You've never known her like this." She raised her head, staring into the distance as she watched what had transpired over the last three days play in my mind. When she finished, she turned to me. "That was not Kali that you handed over to them."

"I assure you, it was. I'd know her anywhere." I clasped my hands, waiting for the weather to change. It would come soon. It always did. When the goddess of destruction returned, we'd all know it. I just didn't know how long we'd have before she'd fully descend into the behavior that earned her the title.

We'd lived countless lifetimes as friends. We'd lived countless lifetimes as enemies. We'd lived countless lifetimes as lovers, and only a few of those were even happier times. Each story had the same ending, though I'd tried to change it despite our fraught history.

Eventually, her nature couldn't be tamed. The devil priestesses—her *family*—groomed and raised her to be what she was. They encouraged Kali to answer the call that drove her into darkness, urging her to drink in the power that came when she was worshipped. As she gained in strength, so did her priestesses. They fed from her, fueling their own influence over the shifters of Arcadia, reveling in the blood that paved the way to their own immortality.

They prepared Kali each and every time so that they, her priestesses, would be revered for their hold over her. Kali was a means to an end. When tribes fought back, or refused to bow before the peacocks, they used Kali's wrath to destroy the realm. I hated them for it.

"You misunderstand, Pan. Yes, it *is* Kali's body, but that's not her mind. Maybe not even her soul. The physical body is merely a vessel, after all," Flora said gently, tilting her neck slightly as she considered saying more. "And you are not following your heart."

"Like a dumbass," her sister chimed in.

"My heart has led me down this path before, Fauna," I argued, though a part of me smiled at her candor.

"More lies," she scoffed, giving me the side eye.

I knew she was right. They both were. That didn't stop my heart and head from battling.

I'd spent three days with a woman unlike any I'd ever known. Brief pieces of the personality I was accustomed to shone through this new version of her, yes. A hardness and an unyielding perseverance were present, but not because she'd been raised by the zealots. She'd been raised by a family. Suffered hardships. Endured loneliness and bullying, but also experienced unconditional love. Joy. Fear.

She'd been shaped by compassion. Humanity, as she'd called it.

It was why she'd cried amid the temple ruins. Why she'd reacted with such anger over having to kill a child, even if it had been in self-defense. It was why she helped bury them.

Those parts of her were genuine. Every bit of her I'd experienced the last three days was a woman I'd never met in all my lifetimes with her.

Her anger was just. Her pain was real. Her love for her family was palpable. She'd made me promise to stop them from searching for her. Her last wish was to protect them.

When she'd looked at me, accepting that I'd traded her life for Flora and Fauna, I saw forgiveness in her eyes. It was an understanding. This version of her didn't forgive easily, but Adora was *capable* of it. In all the eons we'd existed, Kali had never forgiven anyone.

Dark clouds gathered, rolling into each other and blacking out the sky. Rumbling thunder sounded after violent cracks of lightning splintered across the heavens.

I stood, preparing to dive into the water. "Stay here."

"What are you doing?" Flora asked quickly, jumping on all four paws.

"He's going to get Kali," Fauna answered with a knowing smirk I could hear in her voice, not bothering to move.

"No, I'm going to save Adora."

I just hoped I wasn't too late.

CHAPTER 12
ADORA

Darkness enveloped me.

Dreams swirled in my mind, painting pictures that felt like distant memories, each with a red filter distorting the images.

Lifetimes. Childhoods. Births. Deaths. Rebirths.

Visions of pasts being raised by the priestesses. No affection or reassurance. No guidance on right and wrong. Only retaliation. Reminders of my worthiness and what I was *owed* by this world.

Preening when Arcadians gave me what I wanted.

Reverence. Adoration. Worship.

All the while, anger and an all-consuming rage bubbled beneath the surface of my existence, and my self-serving guardians greedily stoked the flames. I watched countless rebirths that led me to indescribable powers. *Destructive* powers. The priestesses urged me to claim my revenge. To show my strength and punish those who refused me . . . those who refused *them*.

In the background, a familiar face always watched from the shadows. A tormented soul wallowing in the anguish

my actions caused him. Crying out for his people. Sometimes crying out for . . . me.

Pan.

My consciousness whispered his name in my mind. A
tender touch grazed my psyche. I felt . . . desire. Regret.
Longing.

Lifetimes together. Fighting. Fucking. Embracing.
Damning.

Each ended the same. My final vision in each life was
his face. His eyes, always filled with the torturous burden of
killing me when he failed to change the course that had
been set. The overwhelming sorrow he felt when he'd lose
me not only to myself, but to the priestesses. My teachers.
My guardians. My groomers. Emotion leaked from his eyes
when he'd whisper his final goodbyes. His apologies. His
failures. His promise that he'd never stop trying to save me.

A flutter in my chest pressed against a cage of bone.

A thousand lifetimes flashed before my eyes, and it was
always the same story. Rage, destruction, and murder. My
death. My rebirth.

But one more story lingered, its uniqueness burning
brighter than any other as the veil of red lifted. My tiny
hand holding my sister's while we played in the creek by
our cabin as little girls. Her smiling face, the light
sparkling in her icy blue eyes when she looked at me.
Fighting together side by side to protect each other. My
sister's wolf nudging me with her snout, helping me
stand when I'd been knocked down. My mom and
stepmom holding me, stroking my hair, offering comfort
and security. Twenty-five years with my family, and it
wasn't enough. It never would be. I was encouraged,
supported, beautifully flawed, and, above all, loved
beyond measure.

An incredible ache consumed me, and my body jolted as though I'd been shocked.

I grabbed the sides of the basin and pulled myself up, breaking the surface and gasping for air.

My eyes shot open, and the ceiling came into view.

"I remember," I choked out.

Turning my head, the three priestesses became my focus. The last thing I had heard before they'd suspended me above the tub and sliced open my throat was the chanting. The room was now silent.

"Rise, Kali, and take back this realm from the wicked," Gold entreated, raising her arms.

I stood, blood streaking down my body in rivulets, returning to the tub that was filled with blood, a sacrificial basin that held a piece of me from every lifetime.

A torrent of emotion raged inside me.

I had one objective.

As I stepped over the rim, a form appeared at the top of the stairs, short sword in hand. His wide eyes met mine, and despair slammed into me. We stared at each other for a moment, and his dejection turned into confusion.

"Put your weapon down, you fool," Blue admonished him. "Kali is reborn. Arcadia has fallen, and we will reshape it again. Do not get in our way, Pan. You know this is how it must be."

"Adora, wait, this isn't you—" he started, ignoring the peacock all together.

I held up my hand.

"You don't command me, Pan," I said through clenched teeth.

The righteous smirks from the priestesses made me swell with pride. They were my truest followers. My first worshippers.

The waterfall curtain around the tub called to me. Stepping into the spray, the water washed away the blood from my body, clothes, and hair. Red-tinted puddles pooled at my feet, the last remnants of my past lives.

This was the beginning of another.

I stood there until the water ran clear. Turning, I faced them. The peacocks . . . and Pan.

A glint of steel shimmered from an altar, catching my eye. It was the very blade they'd used every time I was reborn, forged by the priestesses themselves. But it was my blood forged into the metal. That was what gave it its power. Not them.

Me.

I felt it coursing through my veins. Electrical currents buzzing with excitement. This was my world. I had everything. I had the power I craved after living such a powerless life. The ability to protect myself. To protect my sister. To end those that had harmed us.

"Come, Kali," Gold said, approaching me. "Your return is long overdue."

Taking in her form, my gaze shifted to Blue and Green. I gestured for them to come stand next to their sister. It wasn't a request. Kali didn't make polite suggestions to her followers. I made demands . . . and I would make them bow before me.

Pointing to the ground, it was clear what I wanted. They kneeled, bowing their heads down in reverence. I glanced up to see Pan, and his features hardened. He shook his head, his eyes glazing over.

If he didn't kneel, it was no matter. I would get what I wanted in the end.

"Thank you for bringing me back, my priestesses." I

spoke softly, but in the vast silence of the cursed tomb, my voice echoed in the chambers.

Green smirked, though she kept her gaze down. "As we said, Kali. You always forgive us."

Grabbing the Gold priestess by the hair, I jerked her head back and stared into her wide eyes. Leaning in closely, I whispered, "I never said I forgave you."

I threw my hand out and called to the sacrificial dagger. My magic reached for it, pulling it to me as easily as I might tug an invisible string attached to it.

Faster than they could react, I slit her throat, whispering an ancient chant—old magic that only I knew, and it would ensure her death.

Green and Blue drew back in response, shouting and pleading with me to stop.

I walked toward them slowly while they crawled away. Memories of that decimated temple and the bones of countless children flashed in my mind. I threw the dagger, and it landed with a sickening thud in between Blue's shoulder blades. She crashed forward.

Leaning back, I kicked out hard, concentrating my power into the ball of my foot and breaking Green's femur as she scrambled away. The crunch of her bone was like music to my ears.

Screams filled the room as she tumbled to the ground, curling herself into a whimpering, broken ball, and all I did was laugh.

I called the blade back to me, and it slid out of Blue's back as she cried out.

"Kali, no," she mumbled, her eyes shifting to see me as her cheek pressed against the stone floor. "I ... I can't ... move ..."

"What you can't do is control me." I leaned over her,

smiling as I yanked her head up by her hair, exposing her throat. "I am not yours to command."

Blood poured from her neck after I sliced across her delicate skin and the life drained from her eyes.

Green gasped, crying out for mercy as she rolled over onto her back, trying to back away from me while her mangled leg dragged behind her.

"We can rebuild this world, Kali," she begged.

"Tell me you love me," I said, standing over her.

"You know I love you, my Queen. I would do anything for you."

"Tell me you worship me above all others."

"You know I do. Everything I have done has always been for you."

"Tell me you would kill for me. Anyone that would go against me. Man, woman, or child. Anyone who would dare try to love or worship another."

"I would make them suffer for it, Kali."

"Tell them you're sorry," I whispered.

"What?" Green shook her head fervently. "Please, my goddess, I appeal to your better nature as your most loyal servant."

"I don't have a better nature."

"Give me a chance," she cried out, coughing on her tears.

"Pray to me for forgiveness for what you've done." Rage boiled deep within me, unabating. I thought of the little hands. The tiny finger bone.

"I beg of you, my goddess, please forgive me. I will always serve you."

Kneeling down in front of her, I nodded softly. I reached out my hand and she flinched, but all I did was caress her cheek. "I know," I whispered. "That's the problem."

I shoved the blade into her throat as her eyes widened and bulged. Her mouth popped open, but no sound came out save the gurgling of the blood collecting in her throat.

I shoved her away from me, keeping hold of the dagger. Standing up, I turned to Pan.

"I'm taking this world back," I told him. "And there is nothing you can do to stop me."

PAN

I HAD TO KILL HER. I KNEW IT. IT WAS MY ONLY CHANCE. THE temple stood, and always would, but its priestesses were dead. They couldn't bring her back. Only I knew how.

It would be my responsibility to end her.

To end this.

Yet, I stood frozen, wavering in indecision. For one reason, and one reason only. Not because I loved her. That was a given.

It was because from the moment I crested the stairs and witnessed her rebirth, as I had done so many times before, I sensed the atmosphere had changed. Despair ripped me apart when I saw her emerge from the blood rite. I'd missed my chance to save her. Save Adora. Not Kali. Then, as my hope drained away, I realized I felt Adora's energy. The connection that had been growing exponentially between us was still present. This was the same woman I'd dropped off—a woman unlike any version before. That had to count for something. In every lifetime she was reborn, her wrath returned with a burning intensity. Her power radiated from her in violent waves. Not this time. Power, yes. Violence, yes. Wrath, oh yes . . . but not directed at Arcadia. It was for *them*. The priestesses.

She stared at me; dagger drawn. I returned her gaze, my short sword raised. Silence swelled between us.

I didn't know what to do. I had to stop Kali from her destructive rampage. But I didn't know if I could kill Adora. Love and logic warred within me, and logic even warred with itself.

"What have you done?" I asked, glancing at the corpses of the zealot peacocks.

"Given Arcadia my first gift," she answered with a shrug.

"Your first gift?" I repeated back to her slowly, watching her every move with eagle eyes. She'd slaughtered them with a smile. That was the Kali I had always known. My heart sank when that reality set in.

"Those priestesses will never control me again. They'll never use me again. They'll never urge me to do their bidding again. If I'm going to kill someone, it'll be on my terms. I make my own decisions."

I nodded slowly, breathing out. So that was it. We were back where we'd always ended up.

She saw the resignation on my face and her features hardened. "You still think I'm going to turn into a batshit crazy goddess."

"The thought had crossed my mind, yes," I said.

"Well I'm not."

"And yet you just said you were taking this world back and there was nothing I could do to stop you." The energy coming from her conflicted with her words, but I still felt Adora's presence. Not Kali's.

"I was being dramatic, Pan," she huffed. "It's a fucking

dramatic moment. Technically, yes, you can stop me. Those psychos used me. That won't happen again."

"And what of you taking the world back?"

"I saw what Kali is capable of—what I am now capable of. I held those bones in my hand. Felt the souls that haunt that damned temple. Now I remember *causing it*, but the memory feels more like a nightmare. That isn't *me*. I can't undo any of it. I can't right any of those wrongs, but I can help fix it."

I raised my eyebrow in question, and she glanced at my weapon that I still held firmly in my hand.

"Fix it?" I asked.

"If you'd let me, yeah. I know Kali did nothing but destroy, but I want to help repair the damage she's caused in Arcadia. I've always felt a pull to something greater, and something unknown. Like I'd never belonged on Earth to begin with. I just didn't know what it meant until now. I didn't know about you and this world. I didn't know about my past, but I know who I am deep down inside, and it's not *her*. That shit ends here."

There was a lot she'd wanted to say, and she had the floor. She'd more than earned it.

"The rebirth was complete," I commented lightly, wanting to see how she'd respond.

"Don't I know it." She shuddered.

"That means you're a goddess again."

"I've always been a goddess," she said, shrugging playfully.

"That is not what I meant."

"Yeah, but it's still true in both senses. Kali doesn't live within me, but she is a part of me. Do you understand? *This* goddess"—she swept her hand over her body—" has never existed before." She sighed, throwing her dagger down.

"Look, I know you're capable of killing me. You've had to do it every lifetime I've lived. I also know I can't stop you if you decide you can't let me leave this temple."

The weapon clattered to the floor, and she didn't look at it again.

"What are you doing?"

"The only thing I can do. I'm not going to fight you. Never again. This is me, Pan. The real me. Unindoctrinated, uninfluenced, unfiltered, and true to myself. Take it or leave it. If you're going to kill me, get on with it. You owe me that much. Save your people and put an end to this lifetime."

"And if I let you live? If I go against what every lifetime of yours has told me?"

"I have no idea. Great as my powers are, reading the future isn't one of them. We were bound to each other by a cruel fate, you and me. I know the truth of my creation now. You succumbed to millennia in solitude and begged the fates for a partner. A true equal. They warned you that they would test you. That if you failed, your world would pay a heavy price. You were so lonely, though . . ." Her voice trailed and those brown eyes, ancient as my own, I saw her sorrow. "You took the bargain, but you had no idea that *I* was the test." She looked toward the ceiling, shaking her head. "They made me to be everything you desired. My base nature was and always has been this. Me. But the priestesses, my temple . . . they were my test as much as I was yours. *And I failed.*" She paused, then cleared her throat before speaking again with hesitation. "When my past came back to me and I remembered everything, I had a clarity that I've never had before. In every life, a part of me loved you, but never my whole self. I didn't understand love, so I didn't know what it was when I felt it. The priestesses taught me that vulnerability was a weakness, and I wasn't allowed to have those. I couldn't love you with all of me, not when I didn't even love myself. It was like only a glimpse of my soul was present. I don't know if that means anything to you, but it . . . it was real to me. Even beyond Kali's—my—madness, that was buried inside."

Silence spanned between us. Droplets of water echoed in the quiet darkness of the cave. Her discomfort at my lack of response was palpable. Her eyes shifted, trying to gauge my thoughts. I felt her power tickle the edge of my mind, teasing the edge of my consciousness. She wanted to see my intentions. My truths. I'd kept the shields up around her. For too long she had used it to her advantage, but this time was different. I knew that now.

Her lips parted in a gasp as I removed the block and gave her access to see what she needed.

She saw herself from my point of view. She witnessed the times I loved her more than my world and the times I loved her, even when I hated her. The fights, the fucking, the pain, the sorrow, and the ultimate endings that occurred in every life before. But she saw what she was now. What I could see when I looked at her. That I had already known the truth of who she was. That I loved her more deeply than I had in a thousand lifetimes.

She ran to me, and I dropped my weapon to the side.

Washed clean from the blood of her past lives and sins, Adora wrapped herself around me. Our chests pressed together when she jumped, and I caught her. My hands went to her ass where the tiny shorts that had been driving me crazy for days now had ridden up. I palmed the curve of her, grabbing a handful of what I found there.

Adora groaned. Her arms wrapped around my neck, fingers fisting in my hair. She yanked my head back, looming above me. My lips parted. What she breathed out, I breathed in.

For many lifetimes, I'd been alone. Ones with Kali. Without Kali. They started to blend together when they all ended the same.

Not this time.

Not with Adora.

This was the reincarnation I was waiting for. I knew it as deeply as I knew myself.

Our lips met, tongues twining together—like a thread weaving tightly into an unbreakable bond. Shifter gods didn't have soulmates. Not like shifters.

I had Flora and Fauna to ground me.

Kali always had . . . me.

Until I killed her. Again.

This life would be different.

When the years became long and our immortal life-times never ended, I would be her rock. Her soul when she needed one. Her reminder of who she was.

"If you stop, I swear to every god in the motherfucking realms—"

I chuckled against her, kissing along her jaw. "What makes you think I'm letting you go now, *little peacock*?"

I tested the pet name on my tongue, finding I liked it quite a bit. It suited her. Tiny but with a big personality.

"Thank fuck."

My lips slid down the column of her throat.

I wanted to bite her. Mark her. Suck her flesh between my teeth until it turned red and angry.

Then do it again.

I walked us back to the wall where water poured from crevices in the ceiling. One particularly large break in the stone gushed like a small waterfall. I stepped under it, the cool waters of Atlantis flowing over us.

Liquid ran from her skin to mine as I backed her against the stone wall. Adora gasped when the rough edges touched her spine and I pressed into her front.

My cock was already painfully hard after watching her slaughter the priestesses. Now that I had her warm and wanting, despite my betrayal and the hundreds of past lives between us?

I rolled my hips and the noise that escaped her was nothing short of perfection.

"I need you to do that without clothes," Adora breathed.

I smiled against her temple. The tips of my fingers toyed with the hem of her shorts where her thigh met her cunt. Slick warmth teased me.

"Do you have any idea how difficult it was to not fuck you every time you bent over in these?" I asked her darkly. Her heart rate kicked up, chest moving faster to inhale the air.

"I wanted you to."

I groaned. "That's because your pussy knows who it belongs to, even if it took us a little while to get here."

The corner of her mouth curved into a smirk. A devilish gleam entered her brown eyes. "Does it? Because back in Portal Watch there was this ice fae that was fucking amazing with temperature play and—"

I dragged her from under the spray to the altar in the middle of the room. Her ass smacked against the stone as I dropped her on it unceremoniously. Adora huffed.

I nipped her neck, letting my canines sharpen enough to break the skin. She jumped as my hands came down on her waist to hold her in place.

"You won't be seeing him again." I licked the small punctures, sucking her skin. Adora abruptly arched into me, moaning low.

"You sure about that?" she breathed. "I've got a big appetite."

I stepped back, letting my hands slide over her smooth brown skin to the wet fabric of her shorts. I pinched the hem between my forefingers and thumbs. "I'm sure."

A quick tug was all it took for them to part at the seams. Adora gasped.

"Those are the only pants I have asshole—ahhh!"

I gripped her knees to part her thighs as wide as possible, then kneeled at her feet. The first lick cut her off. The second one had her fisting my hair for a whole other reason.

"You won't be needing them for a while, and when you do, I will make you new ones—that don't show everyone what belongs to me."

She threw one leg over my shoulder, yanking my slick strands while thrusting her hips forward.

I loved her like this. Wild and unrestrained.

"What *belongs* to you?" She was mouthing off, and honestly, I liked it. "Last I checked—"

I licked her ass to slit. The shudder that ran through her turned me on like nothing else.

"What was that?" I growled. The tip of my tongue traced tiny circles around her tight bud. Her thighs tensed, trying to close on instinct. I held them open with ease.

"Keep doing that," she groaned.

"Say it," I demanded. "Say it's my pussy."

Adora tipped her head back. "I don't know. I think you need to do a little more than tease if you wanna be the only one fucking it—"

"*Adora.*"

"*Entitled One,*" she countered right back.

I slid my open palm up her leg as I pulled back, running my lips along her inner thigh. I went slowly, watching her reaction. When I hit a sensitive spot that made her twitch, I bit down hard, marking her with my teeth.

"Fuck," she grunted. "I never said you could bite me. You're going to leave marks everywhere."

I cocked an eyebrow before maneuvering my hand between us so I could shove two blunt fingers into her slick sex. "Hmm," I hummed. "My pussy doesn't seem to mind me marking you."

"Savage," she quipped.

"I am."

If she expected me to be ashamed of that, she guessed wrong.

"I kinda like that," she admitted, breaking off to moan when I curled my fingers to hit a better spot inside her.

"That I'm the god-king and all I want is to fuck this pretty little peacock pussy?"

Adora grunted as her inner walls clenched my fingers. Wetness flooded between her thighs. "Do it."

"Tell me what I want to hear."

Adora groaned. "You're an Entitled Twat—"

I pulled my fingers out and dragged her body to the very edge of the alter so I could slap her pussy with an open palm. Adora's lips parted. A flush began to crawl up her neck.

I grabbed the edges of her shirt and ripped it up the middle. The bra keeping her soft breasts from me was a hindrance. I went to open it with the tiny clasp that was situated snuggly between flawless ocean sand skin.

"Do *not* ruin my only bra on this entire fricken' planet,"

she said as I pinched the clasp and popped it open. The cups flew to either side of her chest, baring her to me.

"You won't need it," I pointed out, my mouth latching onto one of her brown nipples. I licked the raised skin and then sucked it between two teeth, causing the already hard peak to further stiffen with her arousal.

"I'm not a prude, but public nudity isn't really my vibe—"

I bit down, causing the breath to hiss between her teeth.

"I told you; I'll make you new clothes when you need them. Undergarments too." I pulled off her tit with a pop, releasing her angry, swollen nipple. My cock strained harder against my trousers than should have been possible.

"You should put that on a resume. God-king and seamstress." She grinned.

"I don't like seeing marks that aren't mine on you," I murmured, eyeing the reddened skin along the underside of her breast. "I also don't like others providing for you. While we're here, in my world—I will be your provider."

"You know I'm a big girl. I can take care of myself."

I smiled, circling her other nipple with my tongue. "I'm aware, little peacock. I will do these things because I want to, not because you need me to. Let me."

She seemed to consider this, staring at me through shrewd eyes as I toyed with her body. "When we go to Earth to visit my family, will you let me provide for you?"

"Yes," I answered without hesitation. "I am taking you as my mate, Adora. I have no problem with you taking care of yourself. I simply won't share you with others." My response must have quelled some unknown worry because her expression softened.

"You're so sure and yet you've only known me days."

"I've known you for eons. Every version. Every life. This one is different. *You* are different, and it is only *you* that I want. Will you give me that?"

I sucked her nipple between my lips, pulling the blood to the surface. On a shaky moan, my little peacock signed her fate. "*Yesss.*"

A growl of satisfaction ran through me. Possessiveness bore down with a new intensity. "Then tell me what I want to hear. Whose pussy is this?"

I rubbed my fingers through her wet slit.

"Yours."

Mine.

"And what does it want?"

"You inside me," she answered on a breathless sigh as my middle finger lazily traced her nub.

"Ask nicely for it."

"Wh—" She broke off before finishing. Lust was already glazing over her expression, but a new fire lit her pupils aflame, blowing them wide. "Please fuck your pussy."

Music to my fucking ears.

Her jaw clenched, and I slid a finger into her tight channel, loving the grip that immediately enveloped me.

Adora widened her legs, spreading herself to the point it was obscene. I lived for it. My goddess. My temptress.

I used my other hand to undo the laces on my trousers. I loosened them until I could completely free myself. My hard length made the job easier, pushing the fabric down as it sought out her warm heat.

Adora's eyes flicked down then back up, licking her top lip.

I pulled my hand away from between her thighs and pressed my fingers to her lips. She didn't wait for me to tell her to suck, she took my fingers between her lips and licked every trace of herself from my skin like the sweetest honey. "I'm going to fuck this mouth next, but I'd hurt you if I took that first."

Arousal spiked in her gaze.

Her lips popped as she pulled off my fingers with a wet smack.

"Don't threaten me with a good time," she purred.

I lined up my cock with her entrance and thrust once, filling her until I bottomed out. Her back arched off the altar as a strangled sound escaped her throat.

I gripped the soft flesh at her hip, holding her still so I could power into her. Heat covered me as her muscles strained to grip me. Her petite size struggling and yet simultaneously perfect for me in every way.

"Fuck," she cursed, her face contorting. "I'm not ready to be a parent. Not even for dick." She swallowed; face stricken.

I slowed my movements but didn't pull out. "You won't."

She put her hands against my chest. "You're changing your tune from yesterday awfully fast now. My sister may want a tiny tyrant running around and dictating her life but I'm not about that. I want to be the cool aunt. I like sleep and fucking, not to mention silence."

I lowered my head against hers, closing my eyes. My cock twitched in impatience, but I held myself back.

"You're no longer a shifter. You're a god of this world. My equal in every way." She jerked, pushing against my chest in a panic. I grabbed both her wrists, holding her still. "No life would be able to grow inside you without your permission now. You can't get pregnant unless you want to. Think about your past lives. Search the memories. They're all there."

Adora stilled, doing just that. The fight drained away about forty-five seconds later as she let out a deep breath. "Oh, thank fuck. I was worried we'd be all oral for life—which isn't horrible. I mean, there are condoms, but those break and to be honest, I hate them. I might as well be fucking a plastic bag. I've done the only oral before when I was with a snake shifter who had a wicked tongue, but I really like dick—"

My chest rumbled as a deep laugh ran through me. "Every life you've led, you didn't want a child. The reasons always varied, but because of that, we've never had one. If this life is no different, then so be it."

She kissed me hard, biting my bottom lip. "I'm not saying never. Just . . ." She pulled back a fraction and caressed my jaw with her lips. "Give me time. I'm young. I want to live, preferably for a long fucking time before thinking about that."

"You have all the time in the world. Yours and mine. I'm not going anywhere." I took her mouth again, slowly rolling my hips to test the waters. She leaned into me, hands curling in passion as her nails pressed into my shoulders.

"Fuuuuuck. You're so deep like this."

I groaned, relishing her words. "Tell me what you need to get off."

"Choke me."

I wrapped my hand around her throat, pressing my thumb into the divot where it was softer. A slow red spread up her chest as I rolled my hips again, driving into her while pushing against her clit over and over.

Liquid gushed from where we were joined as her first orgasm tore through her.

Her legs wrapped around my waist, bare heels pressing into the small of my back. Crimson stained her skin as her chest rose and fell rapidly. I was on the cusp of release and holding myself off for her.

The next second her pussy contracted, tightening impossibly more. Just as her cheeks started to turn plum-colored, I loosened my hold on her throat. Her lips parted as she sucked in air on a heavy gasp; pure ecstasy written all over her.

I growled, letting the beast in me slip the collar as my pleasure heightened with every second she came on my cock. A scream consumed her, one that I might have thought to be pain, were it not for her shaking legs.

I pushed harder, thrusting till our hipbones slapped. The wet noises of my body meeting hers mingled with my animalistic grunts and her savage moans.

Her convulsing pussy slickened further, and her orgasm sent me flying over the edge. I thrust shallowly twice, before stilling.

"Keep doing that to me, and my pussy is definitely yours," she murmured, pressing her forehead against my chest while she tried to catch her breath.

"I know it is." A rumble in my chest made her smile.

"Cocky," she hummed playfully. Glancing down, she looked back up to meet my gaze. "About my clothes, Mr. God-king seamstress . . ."

As we swam out to the edge of Atlantis, Flora and Fauna sat regally on a stone near the water's edge.

Upon our approach, they each inclined their heads slightly. "Your Majesties."

Adora scrunched her eyebrows while she pulled herself out of the water. "I think you're confusing me for my sister. Which has never happened, by the way. Just call me Adora."

They chuckled, giving me knowing looks.

"The air is shifting," Flora said, scenting the air. "I felt the end of the priestesses, but now Arcadia feels it too."

"Does this mean the shifters that were . . . stuck . . . are they returning to themselves? Their abilities?" she asked, tilting her head to the side, and wringing the water from her hair.

I smiled at her. "It does. It's already happening." I closed my eyes and took a deep breath. "I can feel them. They're happy. Relieved. Somewhat confused, though. We have a lot of work to do."

"And the madness? Is it truly gone?" she asked. The hesitancy in her voice caused the question to come out slowly.

"Diminishing."

Adora looked at Atlantis, half-sunken into the water. Her temple. The place she'd selfishly demolished and yet, preserved for her rebirths. The place only she had the power to destroy. She held out both hands and closed her eyes. Electricity crackled all over her body. The ground began to shake, sending ripples over the sea. The ruins shook as a heavy force pressed against it, splitting the stones, and they tumbled and spilled into the water. Like it was pulled from underneath, the temple sank below the surface, crashing and sending waves to pummel the shore.

When the dust settled, she exhaled a shaky breath, then whispered, "We did it."

"I believe *you* did it. I just stood and watched." I crossed my arms. "Which was incredibly hot, by the way."

"Do me a favor," she said, but trailed off and let her question hang for a moment. "Promise me you won't ever find a way to bring me back to godhood if I die. I know that I'll physically be reborn, but Kali doesn't need to be awakened. Let the goddess within me die too."

"With the priestesses gone, I'm the only one that knows how to bring Kali back, and I swear to you I won't do it." Adora looked at me with relief, but a hint of anxiety appeared on her features. "Do you know what will happen to you if you die now that you've brought down the temple?" She shook her head. "When great injustices occur, you're reborn as you were before. A 'measly' peacock shifter."

"Really? That's it?" she asked, the light sparkling in her eyes. I nodded. "That's not so bad. Lived my entire life as a 'measly peacock shifter'," she said with a wink.

"I figured you'd be okay with it."

"Promise me one more thing." I glanced at her, raising an eyebrow in question. "If that happens, promise to find me again, *love me again,* so I can remember who I am and can always be by your side."

She looped her arms around my waist, and I held her against me. With my lips hovering over hers, I whispered, "I swear it."

I kissed her and felt her smile against my mouth.

"We have one more really big thing to deal with . . ."

"What's that?"

"Going back to Earth and introducing you to my moms. And my sister. And her vampire king-mate."

I raised my eyebrows and breathed a sigh. "Well, after

every lifetime we've shared, that is something I'd never expected to hear."

"C'mon. It'll be fun. Imagine: Family dinners. Holidays. Maybe playing with a niece or nephew soon. Paying my sister back for how awful she is every time she goes into heat by having loud sex in her house." She trailed off, looking at me with trepidation. "What? Too much? Too fast?"

I chuckled. "Not at all. Honestly? I can't wait. The sooner, the better." Adora's smile widened in excitement, and I leaned down to nibble her earlobe and whisper, "I've not had my fill of you yet."

The End.

Thank you again for reading!